STUNNER

This book is a work of fiction.
Names, characters, organizations,
places, events and incidents are
either products of the author's
imagination or are used
fictitiously.

Colin J Galtrey

AUTHOR

1

STUNNER FIVE

STUNNER FIVE

Book number five in the best-selling Stunner Saga. Originally it was just going to be a one-off book but the amazing demand for more from my readers made it impossible to stay at one book. To all of you thank you so much for your loyal support it is very much appreciated.

Now read on in the next blockbuster installment about Saron, Julie and Helen and there unswerving ability to entice danger, romance, wealth, fun times and most of all good friendship.

As they say, "All for one and one for all" Enjoy.

STUNNER FIVE

www.colingaltrey.co.uk

Instagram: thepeakdistrictauthor

Facebook: Colin J Galtrey
(Author)

You tube: Colin J Galtrey

STUNNER FIVE

When then night has been too
lonely,

And the road has been too long,

And you think that love is only,

For the lucky and the strong.

Remember this my friends,

The strong always survive.

Saron XXX

STUNNER FIVE

Chapter 1

Like all things in life, as you get older, you get wiser. You know from reading about me last time how my life was topsy-turvy, then I met Fabio, the day we married was such a joyful day I felt like a Princess. Fabio, what can I say? An incredible human being, loving, considerate, kind. I could go on, but I feel like the cat that got the cream the day he walked into my life.

So, after a fabulous wedding, we are now in beautiful Cuba for three weeks, and I am sat on a beach writing this in my diary. The next bit, you won't believe. "Come on, Saron, let's go for a swim". Yes, you got the voices, Helen and Julie!! They decided to come with us, which you may

think is bizarre, but we are so close. Julie said she needed a break from Tom, who was always one hundred miles an hour and never shut up about his Brits Abroad business. I thought it was starting to bore Ju. On the other hand, Helen finished with her army guy at the wedding. She was utterly smashed and told him he wasn't her type, typical Hells Bells, straight to the point.
I love them both, and Fabio didn't mind. He said whatever makes me happy, dream girl. I can't believe this is the fifth book, and yes, I am deliriously happy and in love.
That evening, Helen had this mad idea for us to go paragliding. I could see Ju wasn't really up for it, but you know Helen, once she

gets a madcap notion in her head, there is no stopping her. Fabio said he was staying at the hotel. He wanted to watch his beloved Brighton play Manchester City, so off we set to the beach at Varadero, it was so lovely. So, there's me in my Baywatch red bikini strutting my stuff, and the guy selling the paragliding experience was a dark tanned Cuban, quite good looking with a great body.

I know he clocked me. He said we could go up on our own, or he would strap himself to us. Well, I wasn't going for having that option. He wasn't going to bloody fixate on me, hoping to join the five-mile-high club. Helen seized the opportunity. Me and Ju saw our chance. "Ok, we will try that

Tiki Bar. Meet us after you have
done the paraglide Helen".

Helen knew what she was doing,
"I'll feel safer if I was with you,
Alejandro", and she winked at Ju
and me. We both laughed, she
was such fun, always up for a
good time.

"Two, sex on the beach Julie
called to the old guy behind the
bamboo bar. "You up for it
tonight Ju"? "Yeah, I fancy a
good drink". We waited for
Helen until 10.30 pm then told
Eric behind the bar, well, that's
what we christened him after five
cocktails, that if Helen came
looking for us, we would be in
one of the bars heading back to
the hotel. We thought there was
little chance of seeing Helen that

night, she had designs elsewhere with paragliding man.

We had another few drinks then the last one in the hotel, Fabio had been watching the match, sadly, he said they had been hammered five nil but typical Fabio, he said he had expected it. That night he seemed a bit distant. "Are you ok Fabio"? "Saron, I have a problem, have you heard of the Jewish Combat Survivors Organization or CS as they call themselves"? "No, who are they Fabio"? "They are a right-wing group who formed after the war to chase down Nazi's, and not just high-ranking officers but any SS officers, they have no interest in putting them before a court, they just kill them and any family they have".

"Oh, that's dreadful". "Yes, they
say they must pay for the sins of
their fathers".
 "What is this to do with you"?
"My father, when he turned
eighty years old, sat me down
and told me about the war and his
involvement. My father was a
Nazi in the SS, although later in
life he renounced his past life.
Dad married an Italian, my mum,
her name was Theresa Caleene.
Dad told her everything so when
I was born, they called me Fabio
Caleene. You remember Bollo
and Maria? She is actually my
sister, we never advertise because
of the CS. I have another sister
who lives in Naples, her name is
Sophia, but we have had no
contact for many years, again,
because if the CS found dad, then

the whole family are in danger.
Dad is ninety-seven and tonight I
got an email from a frightened
Bollo, he said they had found
dad, he had been beaten then shot
four times, his modest house was
ransacked looking for addresses
of any family. They are highly
organized Saron".
"You said your dad was in the
SS, what was his role"? "His
name was Franz Groopon, before
the war he had been a doctor, but
he was made to join up and was
injured on the Eastern front so
was sent to Garipol Workers
Camp, but it was really a death
camp. There he was assigned the
job of choosing who was fit for
work and who would go straight
to the showers, or as we now
know, the gas chamber. Until

mum fell ill, I never spoke to my father after he'd told me what he had done, then mum died, and he became frail, and I didn't have it in my heart to be cruel to him. When we became close again, that's when he told me about the CS. The CS see the punishment for anybody involved to be the same as they felt losing their families. We knew about this in the Service, but they are mega secretive, and we had tried many times to infiltrate them, but we lost three operatives so that idea was shut down". "What happens now Fabio? I don't scare easily but you sure are concerning me. If I am understanding this correctly, I am now part of your family, therefore, that makes me a target". "I'm sorry Saron, it wasn't anything I thought about but now it's reality. I'm not philosophical but I will say this, it is what my father said to me. "Not all men are born equal, some are born rich, some brave, some are leaders, some lucky and some stupid". My father told me I was brave and that he had been stupid. I never quite understood what he meant until one day, I was on a top-secret mission, and I was captured. My dad had always said I had to be brave, even as a little boy, so the day I was captured his words were ringing in my ears. I was held and tortured for five days but it felt like fifty days. The mission was to take out a drug lord, but what we didn't know was, one of our team of four was on his payroll. It was dreadful Saron, but I did escape and whilst the threat from CS is real, I doubt they will come after you, more likely they will follow the bloodline, but I can protect you". "Fabio, you are so kind, it's really hard to believe you worked for the Secret Service". "The reason for telling you all this is I need to go to my father's funeral, and I also have to figure out how I look after my sister Maria and her husband Bollo and then to try and find my sister in Naples". "I'll come with you". "No, it could be too dangerous, stay here in Cuba with Julie and Helen until the end of the holiday then, once I have sorted my family, we can settle down in Cornwall"

STUNNER FIVE

That night, Fabio flew home. I told the girls his sister was poorly, I didn't want to frighten them, they had both been through so much with me and especially Julie. Helen had copped off with the paragliding guy so me and Ju decided to stop overnight in Havana with a trip from the hotel. It really was fascinating, just like you see on the telly, all the old cars and women rolling Havana cigars on their thighs.

That night we went to a show, which wasn't brilliant but for what we paid for the trip we couldn't complain. The rest of the holiday we hardly saw Helen, she was all loved up, but we did hit the bars on the last night, my head the next day felt like there was somebody inside it with a

jack hammer and my mouth
tasted like the bottom of a budgie
cage. Ju was the same, but Helen
was in fine form.
We knew going back that there
were things to do before we
opened but I was hoping by then
my lovely Fabio would be back
and we could have a normal life
in Cornwall. Guess my life isn't
meant to be straight forward
After we landed it was another
three weeks before I heard
anything from Fabio, but it wasn't
Fabio, it was a very frightened
Bollo. He said Fabio had taken
Maria, but he couldn't leave
Sardinia as his mother was very
old and she was all he had. He
said Fabio thought that they
would go after Maria because of

the bloodline but that me and
Bollo might be ok.

Why can't just have a normal
life? I thought. I decided to fly
out to Sardinia to try and calm
poor Bollo. Like always, I am
drawn to danger, I don't know
what it is but I am. The girls were
busy getting the café bistro ready,
so it was maybe an ideal time.
They knew I was concerned
although they didn't know the
real truth, so they didn't question
me too much.

I drove to Heathrow then got a
flight to Sardinia and picked up a
car and told Bollo I would meet
him at Pula with its wonderful
beaches and archeology. Bollo
was on time, but he looked so
worried, all the time we were
talking he was looking around

him. "Saron this isn't safe for
you. I know Fabio thinks because
we are not bloodline they will
leave us alone but I read a case
on the internet where they state
the severity of the crimes that
they are avenging and they wiped
out sixteen people of one family
whose grandfather had been a
Kapo at Buchenwald in charge of
the gassings at one of the
showers, he survived the war and
nobody knew what he had done
but then a newspaper article
came out about the evil things the
Kaps did to their own people and
this old man had a breakdown
and confessed to a nurse in the
nursing home. Within two days
he was dead and within five
months his whole family had
been murdered so, no, we are not

safe Saron, Fabio is wrong this time".

"What are you going to do"? "I am going into hiding, I need time to work this out and if you are sensible, you will do the same Saron". Bollo finished his coffee and said, look after yourself then he kissed me on my cheek and scurried away. Charming I thought, I've flown all this way for a cup of coffee and a horror story.

It was clear my life was in danger, so it was decision time. Do I follow the man I love or go home and take my chances? Mum always used to say, "You come into this world alone lass and you will go out of it alone" So, decision made I'm going home. I booked the flight for the

next day and, If I am honest, I
was on edge, every face seemed a
potential threat. The next day at
the airport while waiting for the
plane, the news was reporting a
man had been found dead with
his head in a gas oven although I
was struggling to understand, the
picture was of Bollo! They were
saying it was suicide, but I knew
different. They were onto us; the
plane could not come quick
enough; these men were ruthless.
I landed back at Heathrow and
drove back to Cornwall with
some haste. I had no idea where
Fabio was and even if he was
alive or Maria or his other sister.
Bollo was dead and there was a
chance they were coming for me.
The girls were surprised to see
me and, of course, over a bottle

of wine, the questions were coming thick and fast, and it was important they knew everything. Ju listened intensely, Helen on the other hand was full of questions like a special agent.

It was 4.00 am and three bottles of red wine later when we decided to call it a night. The following morning at breakfast the girls said I should go away for a short time or until Fabio comes back. To be honest, they were right, but I think Fabio won't be back. Julie said she had an aunty in a place called Sutterton in Lincolnshire, her husband had died, and she had a three bedroomed small holding and would welcome the company. Julie said, "Do you want me to call her Saron"?

"Yes, please Ju". Julie picked up the phone. "Aunty Emily its Julie". "Hello love how are you"? "I'm good thank you". "Bet you are busy getting the place ready for the season". "Yes, we are aunty Emily". "How's Saron and Helen"? "Helen's fine but Saron's has been a bit off colour and wondered if she could come and stay with you"?

"Oh, that would be lovely, it's quite lonely since your uncle Arthur passed away love". "So, is it ok if she drives up tomorrow"? "Of course, it is, I haven't seen Saron since she was about thirteen". "Ok aunty Emily, she will be with you around 2 00 pm tomorrow and thank you". "No, thank you, I can't wait for the company".

"It's for the best Saron, you will be safe there". "Thanks Ju, obviously, if Fabio turns up, get him to contact me straight away". "Of course, mate". The following day with my case packed I headed for Sutterton with not a clue about how my life may work out.

Chapter 2

I wasn't apprehensive about staying with Emily, I remember she was a nice lady. I came into Sutterton village, there was a pub and a petrol station on a roundabout but that was about it. The Sat Nav took me down Rowan Thorpe Lane, again, there was nothing, then a farm then another quarter of a mile and the small holding. Emily was stood by the gates to the property and waved me in. I parked on the gravel stone drive. Emily shut the gates then gave me a big hug.

"It's so lovely to see you and still such a pretty girl, you look like your mum did love".

The cottage was white-washed brick with a beautiful wisteria growing over the rear of the cottage. "Here Saron, have a cup of tea and one of my home-made scones then I'll show you around. This is the front of house; Arthur planted these clematis when we bought the place twelve years ago". I could see she missed Arthur but was proud of what they had achieved with their cottage. The garden was immaculate, we followed a little winding path to a small orchard with apple and pear trees, blackberry, and raspberry bushes. "Oh, plums Emily, I love plums" "Then you must try my plum and walnut jam in the morning for breakfast. Now, come and see the animals". "You have animals"? "Oh yes dear, we have Cuthbert the goat, Jayne the Jersey cow and Patricia the pig and her piglets". "This is idyllic Emily". You could help me plant my cauliflowers, you just walk at the back of the tractor and every time you hear a click you drop a plant in the hole made by the tractor. If you would, we could do this tomorrow"? "Yes, great Emily". The following morning, true to her word, Emily had done thick toast and lovely plum and walnut jam.

That night I slept like a log. I was so tired, the fresh air had got to me, the next day I decided to tell Emily why I was hiding out, I felt it was only fair. Emily laughed when I told her, she said she thought I might be hiding from an irate husband! Guess the

real story took some believing so
we never mentioned it again.

I had a good life, it was
very tranquil with walks with
Emily's Dulux dog that she had
named Painter, which I thought
was funny. I felt really relaxed
when I got a call from Julie, she
said her, and Helen were
homeless, there had been a fire in
the café bistro, and it had burned
to the ground. I told them to stay
at my cottage at Polruan and I
would come home next weekend.
I told Emily of my plans and she
said to be careful, and she would
miss me,
It was with a heavy heart that I
left Emily and my peaceful life
but now my friends needed me. I
had heard nothing from Fabio so
didn't know how he was or if he

was still alive? I arrived late Saturday night, the girls were still up watching a film. We hugged and Helen opened a bottle of red wine, we sat at the kitchen table where they told me that the chef had somehow accidentally set fire to the kitchen, luckily, he was just prepping so there was just him Helen and Julie in and they all got out unscathed but the building didn't have the same luck.

"I'll go with you tomorrow and see what we can do, if we have to re-build, we'll do it and make it even better girls" and they chinked glasses. "Welcome back Saron. What are you going to do about Fabio"? "He knows what he is doing, I know Fabio will be prepared, that's the man he is".

STUNNER FIVE

The following day, all three of us had headaches but we set off to see the damage to the property. To say I was shocked would be an understatement, there was very little left, just a pile of bricks.

On the plus side, I had always felt we needed more accommodation so, that afternoon, I sat down and made a list for the girls and arranged to see an architect the following day. We all agreed we would want five bedrooms with en-suite, a forty-seat dining area with big glass windows to take in the view, three en-suite staff rooms and an ultramodern kitchen. The architect said it would take a couple of weeks to get the first drawings to us which was fine, by then the insurance company should have settled. "Right girls let's go into Newquay to celebrate the new plans for our place and Saron being home". "The three Musketeers ride again"! Helen stated. "You do realize we will have a whole year off Helen". "I know, it's not great from a business standpoint but just look at the fun us three could have". "Think you might have to count me out, I'm going to find Fabio". "Well, if you are, we should come with you, shouldn't we Ju"? "Yes, you are not going on your own Saron". "Look, it's really kind of you but it is too dangerous". "We aren't arguing about this are we Helen? We are going with you and that's final".

STUNNER FIVE

It made feel really loved and
quite emotional that I had such
good friends.

We arrived in Newquay and
headed for The Smoked Kipper, a
bar right on the harbour front. It
was full of early doors drinkers,
virtually all men, so you can
imagine the wolf whistles when
the three of us walked in.

We were in there almost two
hours and never had to buy a
drink. When we left, we were
laughing at the different guys that
had been hitting on us. Poor
Helen had the weirdos where Ju
had the heavy drinkers, and I had
the younger lads fancying their
chances, it really was funny. We
had a great night, it was good to
put aside my worries and have a
dance in the Soul Train, a club

owned and run by ex-England rugby captain Todd McClusky who had been trying his patter on me. I asked him how, with a name like McClusky, he had played for England. He explained his father was English but had left his mum when he was about three and she remarried to a Scotsman and took his name and changed his, he said his father's name was Brown.

He was a nice guy but being married wasn't an option, but it didn't spoil the night, we danced plenty then eventually got a taxi back to Polruan. The following day Helen wanted to cook breakfast, she probably was the best cook out of the three of us so me and Ju tried to come up with a strategy to find Fabio. That day, I booked flights to Naples for the three of us in the quest to find him and hopefully he had saved his sister Maria.

At the airport, I could tell Julie and Helen really hadn't got a clue about the danger this trip could have for us all. I was worried I was taking my friends into something more akin to pure evil than a trip abroad which they basically saw it has.

My dad always said his father used to say, "See Naples and Die" which would have meant you would never eclipse the beauty of the place, he had been there during the war. It seemed a poignant thing now because it could be entirely possible that I could see Naples and die!

There I go, being negative again, I need to get my positive head on to be successful. Julie had sorted a hotel called Cappella Sansevero, named after a famous chapel in Naples. It was clean and tidy but not five star plush. We decided to split up and, all armed with a recent picture of Fabio, we set off around the bars, restaurants, and taxis; hopefully, somebody might recognize him. It was the third day with me feeling quite despondent that Julie had some luck. Fabio had been staying at a small hotel. I went to question the receptionist. She said Fabio was a lovely man and that he told her his sister was working in Bella Lasagna restaurant in the square and he was going to see her today. "How

far to the restaurant from here"?
"Maybe three miles". Helen
flagged a taxi, and we headed
there. My heart was racing, but as
we got closer there was
pandemonium. The taxi driver
said police were diverting traffic,
and we had best get out there.
Walking down to the restaurant,
my heart sank. The police were at
the Bella Lasagna. Had the CS
found them? Again, I went cold,
two bodies were brought out on
stretchers in body bags. I broke
through the police only to be
stopped by a detective. I
explained who I was, he said a
man had shot two women. When
I asked what nationality, the
shooter was, he said Middle
Eastern he believed but he had
got away. I knew straight away,

but had Fabio not got there or
had he been taken? That, I didn't
know. The girls tried to console
me saying that maybe Fabio
wasn't there yet or maybe he
escaped. That night in the hotel
the news was on, although, in
Italian. Helen could speak a little
and she said they were saying a
receptionist, Greta Bollinson and
Maria something were killed, we
had waited for over four hours
but no sign of Fabio. I just knew
if he was alive, he would find
me. We spent the rest of the week
in Naples, but I was hardly in a
great place and was pleased to
head back to Cornwall. Most
nights I would wake up thinking
about Fabio, my love, the man I
wanted to spend the rest of my
life with.

Chapter 3

The months dragged on, the new building was taking shape, so my mind was occupied but Fabio was always at the forefront of my thoughts.

I will always remember this day, June 17th , it was a typical English summers day when my phone rang. I didn't recognize the number and normally that would mean I wouldn't answer but this time something was telling me to answer.

"Hello, who is this"? "My name is Mosha, we have Fabio and if you wish to ever see him again you will follow my instructions, are we clear"? "Let me speak to him first". "I give the orders; you are not your ancestors in the camps bitch" he said in a chilling purposeful way.

"You will fly to Tel Aviv, and you will be met by a man holding up a sign with your name, go with him. If you try anything, Fabio is dead. The next flight is tomorrow at 9.00 am, make sure you are on it" and he hung up.

I told the girls and this time I was on my own as I headed for Heathrow. The flight seemed to take an age. I just hoped my

STUNNER FIVE

Fabio was alive and this wasn't just to kill me, whichever way it went I had no choice. Tel Aviv was a modern airport hand luggage was all I took so I was soon in the concourse. I looked and looked but could not see anybody with a board with my name on it. Suddenly, I felt a gun in my back, I dare not turn around, this voice said keep walking. We went to a high-rise car park where they blindfolded me and threw me in the back of a van.

They were arguing between themselves as we drove along, every now and again we would hit a pothole. After about thirty minutes the van stopped, and they dragged me out and took me inside. When they took off the blindfold, I was in a darkened room, it was very smokey, my hands were tied and there were two middle eastern men in the room. The first one said he was Mosha and the second man with a terrible cut right across his face introduced himself as The Goat. "So, you are Saron, wife of Fabio"? I just looked at him with contempt. "Where is Fabio"? They looked at each other. "Fabio needs your help". "I want to see him". "Fetch him Mosha". He came back with Fabio; he had been beaten almost to death. They threw him on the floor in front of me. "What have you done"? "We tried to loosen his tongue, so now we loosen yours, but first we shoot him". "No, stop, what do you want"?

STUNNER FIVE

We know Fabio was MI6 and we also knew you were, so we want the files they have on CS" then the man walked over and calmly put the gun to Fabio's head and pulled the trigger. I screamed and at that point I didn't want to live.

With my whole world seemingly at an end, self-preservation kicked in. "So, Saron, this is the deal, you find the files, you steal the files and our agents let your friends live". "What, and then you kill me"? "Maybe we find a use for you. In your defense, you didn't know Fabio's family history so maybe we let you live".
I didn't know if this was bullshit, they may still kill me but at least I could save Ju and Helen who were innocent in all this.

STUNNER FIVE

They untied me and I fell on my
knees to hold my dear Fabio.
Being the person, I am, I knew
these two would have to pay, I
just didn't know how. "Right, get
up". They threw me a towel and
soap and told me I would be on
the next plane to London, and I
had three months to do what was
asked, on the last day, if I had
cheated them or failed, all three
of us would be killed.
With this prospect it was time for
a charm offense at MI6, my one
hope was to get friendly with Sir
Gavin Clearmont, the top man,
this was going to take all of my
persuasion to try and strike up
first a friendship then build it up
to where he would trust me.
Anyway, one hurdle at a time I
thought as I reported to the front

desk. "Can I help you"? this mid-fifties, snotty nosed cow asked. "Yes, I am here to see Sir Gavin Clearmont". "Do you have an appointment"? I knew if I said no, she wouldn't let me go any further. "Yes, I do". "Who shall I say you are"? Old cow, I thought. "Just say Saron". It was quite common for agents to just give their Christian name so I knew this wouldn't draw suspicion to the stupid cow.

"Just a moment" she rang Clearmont. "Sir Gavin I have a lady called Saron waiting for your meeting. I could tell he hesitated, but he told her to take me to his office.

"Get a pot of tea please Janice" he said to cow bag, much to her displeasure. I had put on a little

red dress, showing my legs off in
all their glory which I remember
Clearmont ogling the last time
we met.

I sat across from him using all
the sexual prowess I could
muster, crossing my legs
numerous times like a scene from
the famous Sharon Stone film.
He was interested, his eyes were
out on sticks! "So, Saron, lovely
to see you, I never expected our
paths to cross again". "Well, I
always had a lot of respect for
you sir" I said, lying through my
teeth. "I was in London and had
an afternoon to kill and thought I
would pop by and say hello". He
clearly could not believe his luck.
"Would you like an early evening
meal? I know a brilliant little
restaurant near my apartment, it's

called Eddies, superb food and service". "Ooh yes, that would be lovely Gavin" I said, crossing my legs, revealing a bit more each time. I had this sucker on my line. I bet you are thinking I'm dreadful, but this is about self-preservation for me and the girls and revenge, eventually, for Fabio. A girl has to do what a girl has to do.

We finished our tea, and he gave me directions to Eddies. I nipped back to the hotel to get changed, I put on a really sexy lingerie set, I was going to win this one, of that, I was sure.

I arrived at Eddies at the time he said. It was a real swanky place, all the waiters wore black shirts and long white aprons folded at the waist, just like in the movies.

STUNNER FIVE

Clearmont was late, I could see by his expression that he had rushed to get to the restaurant. "I am so sorry Saron, something popped up at work, an ex-MI6 operative who had retired was found beaten and shot". I knew straight away he was talking about Fabio and that he had no clue we were married. Just shows how luck can change the course of destiny. "I shouldn't discuss this, but a far-right organization is hell bent on killing surviving Nazis, we believe they did it but why, that isn't so clear. We are looking into Fabio's past". Clearmont stopped himself. "I'm sorry, I shouldn't speak about these things, they are highly confidential. It's just that you make me feel relaxed" he said, ogling my ample cleavage in my wrap around Karen Millen green dress.

"Anyway, have you looked at the menu"? "Yes, I fancy the coriander smashed egg to start and the goat's cheese crispy stack with Amish raspberries". "I'm guessing by what you are ordering you are a vegetarian Saron"? "Absolutely Gavin" I said, giving him even more come on signals. Luckily for me he wasn't a bad looking bloke but if I could avoid sleeping with him that would be the best option. The dinner was very nice, and he was quite good company although he liked to name drop. He said he had been at school with Prince Edward and played polo with most of the Royal

Family. He then said he had been
for dinner with the Blairs, but his
favourite story was about being
invited to Balmoral for Christmas
with the Queen and Prince Philip
about four years back. This guy
was connected but then again, he
would be as head of MI6.
"Are you married Gavin"?
Clearmont coloured up and he
stuttered for words. "It's kind of
difficult, my wife and children
live in the family home Jollycum
Hall in Suffolk but with me based
here in London, we have sorted
of drifted". "Is that the posh way
of you saying you play around
Gavin"? He laughed, "Let's say I
have nothing holding me back
Saron".
"You intrigued me about the
group going around killing

Nazi's, there can't be many left can there"? "This group targets Nazi families and they wipe everybody out. We believe their theory is, leave nobody standing like the Nazi's did to the Jews". "Wow, you must have a room full of information on these people". "Yes, we do and the only access to the room is through the bookcase in my office that has a secret door". "I would love to see that Gavin, it's very James Bond". After that he clammed up realizing he had probably told me too much. But now I knew the next thing I had to do was to speak to CS and find out which files they wanted. We finished the meal and Gavin asked me if I wanted a night cap at his apartment around the corner. I declined but arranged to call him the following week to arrange something.

That night in the hotel I realised I hadn't grieved for the loss of Fabio, and I spent the night sobbing. I would hand out revenge to these evil people, everybody can be assured of that. The following morning, I contacted CS, and they said the main guy was going to meet me at Speakers Corner at 1.00 pm. I arrived at 12.50 pm and waited, it was almost 2.00 pm when a big guy with a goatee beard approached me, he had the two guys with him who had tortured and killed poor Fabio. The guy sat next to me with the big guys behind. "Saron, I am Moshala. What do you have for me"? "MI6 have loads of files on CS. I need to know if you have a specific file you want". "I want two files: the UK Home secretary William Gershwin and the other is Chancellor of the Exchequer Bradley Secombe". "Why do you think they may be filed there"? "Because we believe Gershwin's grandfather was the advisor to Goering and Sercombe's grandfather arranged the transportation for five Nazis to escape to America when the Germans had lost the war". "If you know this, why do you need the files"? "Because the families are in the files and they all must die". "If I do this, I and my friends won't be harmed"? "If that is what we told you then yes". "You must give me time".

STUNNER FIVE

"You have four weeks from today, I will be sat here in four weeks to the day, if you deliver, ok, if you don't then you know the outcome for you and your friends". With his threat ringing in my ears, I returned to my hotel room to figure out a plan. I had seen where Clearmont put the key to the CS room but how was I going to get in there?

The only way I knew was to meet him at his office and somehow drug him. I researched undetectable drugs and the one that fit was Cazaleen, a Spanish drug used for interrogation, it allows the prisoner to be out of it for thirty minutes without any side effects. I worked out the ingredients and to my surprise, I could create it with things off the shelf. You rub it under the nose of the victim and it's almost instant.

I rang Clearmont and told him I had enjoyed myself with him so much I was going to stay in London for another few days.

I could sense the excitement in the idiot's voice. "Great, let's meet up"." I've just got a couple of things to do, and I will call you Gav" I said in an endearing voice.

Right, the plot was now set, now to get the ingredients to make the drug. Like I said, it was incredibly simple, I just had to hope it worked. The following day with the drug made, I rang him, my plan was to have a meal and imply we would have sex but I was going to say it would be a

big thrill to have it in his office,
that way, I would get through
security without the usual checks
as I would be with Clearmont.
We arranged to meet at Covent
Garden at a lovely little intimate
restaurant called Sandos. I called
into a lingerie shop, I needed to
spike his interest and bought a
white basque, white stockings
and a blue garter. I chose the
smallest basque I thought I could
get into making my bust look
even bigger. He was at the table
when I walked in, he straight
away eyed up my shopping bag.
"Victoria's Secrets hey Saron?
Hope it's something for me".
"Down Rover" I said, "Have
patience". The bloody idiot was
like a dog on heat. Me

personally, I just wanted to get
this over with.

We had the meal then I told him
my fantasy about making love in
his office and that was why I had
bought the basque etc. "I'm not
sure Saron" "Ok, forget it then" I
said. "Can't we just go to my
hotel"? "Gav where is your sense
of daring"? "Oh, to hell with it,
nobody dare come into my
office".

He ordered a taxi and we set off.
We just breezed through security,
it was quite a joke really
although, the two guys did notice
the lingerie bag as I smiled at
them.

Once in his big oak paneled
office he pounced on me. "Hey
slow down Tiger, let me get
changed into your present. Can I

go in there"? and I pointed to the
CS file room? He took the bait;
he was that aroused he basically
had lost all his inhibitions. He
unlocked it and said don't be
long. I changed and have to say,
it felt uncomfortable, but it had to
be done. I put the drug on my
finger, when he saw me, he
almost went bow-legged. I didn't
mess about, he tried to kiss me,
and I put my finger to his mouth,
sliding the drug under his nose,
he immediately fell asleep. I
dashed into the room and had
been looking for about fifteen
minutes and was beginning to
panic when I spotted both files, I
took a quick look then stuffed
them in the lingerie bag and
changed. I undressed Clearmont
down to his underpants and left. I

knew he would have no idea
what had happened. I smiled at
the two guards as I left but I did
take a few pictures of him in his
undressed state, just for insurance
purposes you understand
My heart was beating fast, back
at the hotel room I lay on the bed
and read about the two ministers.
First, the Home Secretary,
Gershwin, whose grandfather
was a strategic advisor to
Goering, this would blow the
Government to pieces! It stated
Gershwin had been married to an
Italian, after the war they had two
children who they gave British
names to, Harry and Margaret.
Margaret was killed in a
motorbike accident, but Harry
married Louise Canning, they
had two children, Freddie who is

the Home Secretary's brother and William, the Home Secretary. Freddie had two girls, Jenny and Gwen, so in total, if I hand over these papers and addresses, that would mean Louise, who was still alive, Harry had died a year earlier, then there was William, the Home Secretary, his wife Sandra and their three girls Felicity, Penny and Izzy. That is a lot of people to be murdered, including Freddie, his wife Pamela and their two girls, Jenny and Gwen, that was a total of nine deaths. Then, add to that Bradley Secombe and his wife, also his mother who was still alive, his two children, George and Scarlett, it made a total of fourteen needless deaths that I

would be basically accountable
for, but what else could I do?
 I decided my best bet was to
come clean with Gavin
Clearmont but first I photocopied
the files and the pictures of
Clearmont then stored them in a
safety deposit box in Bond Street.
I then called Julie and told her
the full story in case something
happened to me.
I built up the courage to call
Clearmont and arrange to meet
him, he wasn't happy, but I guess
he wouldn't be. We sat outside a
café in Covent Garden, I felt
safer that way. "So, Saron, what
was that all about the other
night"? I hesitated for a minute
but then, what the hell, I couldn't
have the deaths of all those
people on my conscience and I

had no guarantees they would not kill me Julie and Helen. Clearmont smiled a smug smile. "You do know I should arrest you and they would throw the key away? That is top secret property". "I know you could, but I also know that your career would be over as well would it not"? "Then maybe a second option, where you disappear never to be seen again"? "Mmm, let me think about that, there are strict instructions in place if I don't contact a certain person within ninety days, they will go to the tabloids with pictures of you and the files I stole". This stopped Clearmont in his tracks, he wasn't expecting that, he thought he was dealing with a bimbo!

STUNNER FIVE

"Ok, now the niceties are out of
the way, what do you want"? "I
want you to go after them and put
me and my two friends under
twenty-four surveillance".
Clearmont laughed, "Proper little
Miss Moneypenny aren't we
Saron"? "If you like, but that's
the deal". Ok, well, this has been
needing sorting for a long time.
Oh, by the way, why didn't you
mention Fabio"? "I thought it
would complicate things". "For
what it's worth, he was a good
man and an excellent field
officer. I am sorry for your loss".
Was this a soft side of Clearmont
or because he knew I was holding
all the aces?
"Here, write down what you
know about CS then, once I have
the files back and the pictures, I

will arrange a safe house for you and your two friends". I had to trust him but unknown to him I had copies. "Meet me here tomorrow and I will instruct you".

That night I rang Ju and Helen. "What about the rebuild while we are away"? "It will only be a few weeks" I said but really not having a clue, I just hoped I had done the right thing, only time will tell.

How the hell does this happen to me? After I found Fabio, I really thought my life was sorted and now I have all this crap and my two best friends are implicated, things just don't seem fair. After a bout of self - pity I got my head around what's happening and met him the next day. To be very fair

to Gavin Clearmont, he seemed
to be genuine, I guess only time
will tell. I didn't want to ruin his
career, but I had to have
insurance, our lives were on the
line.

Gavin smiled and kissed my hand
as I arrived at the little street
café. "Right Saron, let's get this
done". I handed him the files and
the pictures I had stolen, of
course, he was unaware I had
copies.

"When this is over, come back
and work for MI6". I just smiled.
"We have a safe house for you
and your friends, it's in County
Clare, Ireland. It's not anything
flash but it's clean and safe. I
have two officers watching you
around the clock, these are your
new identities. You are Laura

STUNNER FIVE

Brush your friends are Amy Chicott for Helen and Samantha Town for Julie. Your friends are being picked up as we speak, and you will meet them in Liverpool for the ferry, we have supplied a car with all the necessary paperwork in your name. I will be in touch". "Thank you, Gavin, but how long might this last for"? "We have done some work on the group and now that they have killed Fabio, an ex-MI6 agent, that was a big mistake for them. I would guess at the most, three months but make sure you follow what the handlers tell you in Ireland. This organization will not go to trial, our mandate is to wipe them off the face of the earth. We don't want other groups springing up. Good luck

Saron and hopefully we can meet
up for a meal when this is over"
and he handed the car keys to a
Fiat 500. No expense spared here
I thought but beggars can't be
choosers. I also had my ticket. I
assumed the girls had theirs.
Gavin left and I tried to phone
Julie but my phone and their
phones were blocked it said. It
was beginning to hit home how
real all this was.

Chapter 4

The ferry was booked for a 2.00 pm crossing. I arrived and parked the car below and set off to the top deck, it wasn't busy so I easily found the girls, they were stood with two guys who introduced themselves as Andy Wilson, he was about six foot two and very athletically built, he looked a bit like Tom Cruise, and the other handler shook my hand, he was about six foot and the first thing I noticed was his teeth, all bright and white, he also had an American accent and said his name was Mark Fresner.

I didn't ask anymore, I thought I would save that until later. We all seemed to get on well, they explained that the house would feel like a prison, if we wanted to go anywhere, a handler would be with us.

This wasn't ideal by a long way, but I had to make Ju and Helen understand our lives were in serious danger. Probably for the first time in my whole life I felt vulnerable and not in control.

After a long journey, we arrived at the safe house in County Clare, it was down a track in a wood. The little house looked like something Hansel and Gretel would have lived in. Andy said it had been a wood cutter's house some years ago, but MI6 had taken it for a safe house. We settled in and Mark said he would do a shop for groceries, and beer of course.

It was quite rough living there, the hot water for the shower would last for about one and a half showers before it went cold then it would be a ninety-minute wait before the next two people had a chance, so we did a rota and took turns.

We spent hours playing monopoly and scrabble and after almost there months we were all going stir crazy, we talked the lads into taking us out for a few drinks, they were as fed up as us.

STUNNER FIVE

It was decided we would go into Lollypandy, a small fishing village where Bert Trumans bar was. Mark said he had done a stint here before and he said only locals got in this bar.

We were like teenagers, doing our make-up and trying on different clothes. Andy said we must dress down as if we were on holiday, just in case. So, we all wore jeans, although mine were the light blue clingy type and I wore a brown mohair jumper that was just on one shoulder. Don't think Andy was too chuffed but hey, you know Saron!

The pub had music on, you know, that fiddly stuff they all play, the problem was the bar only had Jameson's Irish whisky, Guinness and for some strange reason a cloudy cider which I later found out the landlord brewed illegally. They were nice people, and we certainly got some looks. Helen, the beer monster of course, wasn't holding back, the fishermen loved her, so it wasn't a great surprise when she went to the toilet and didn't return. I just thought she is having a snog. Helen wasn't loose in any shape or form, she just let her hair down. Anyway, after twenty minutes or so Andy was getting fidgety and decided to go and look for her. I was on my third pint of this bloody strong cider and to be honest, I felt a bit tiddly. Andy came back looking worried. "What's a matter"? "She isn't there". "What do you mean

not there"? I said. "Not bloody
there Saron, will she have gone
with that fisherman"? "No,
definitely not". "We will lose our
jobs over this Mark. Grab your
coats, we'd better start looking
for her". Like I said, I was a bit
the worse for wear, but I know
Helen and she wouldn't do
anything to put us in danger. We
checked everywhere until it was
dawn, it was like she had just
disappeared without trace. We
ended up going back to the
cottage in case she had walked
home but there was no sign.
Now I was worried. Andy
phoned Clearmont and I could
hear his raised voice bawling out
Andy and Mark. When the call
ended, I asked Andy what he
said. "You are being moved; the

cottage has been compromised". "I'm not going anywhere without Helen". "This isn't a choice, Saron. Get your stuff and get in the car, you too Julie". Andy meant it, we didn't have a choice, he said Mark would stay behind to try and find Helen, but we were going back to London. We both sobbed, what if they had Helen and were torturing her? I knew this was a massive mistake. At MI6, Clearmont told us we were going to the island of Jersey where we would be able to blend in with it being a holiday island, he said we would be met at Jersey Airport by agent Graham Stokes and agent Phil Stanz. "What about our friend Helen"? Clearmont seemed agitated. "We are doing everything to find her

Saron, but you must follow the rules, or you will jeopardise your safety and that of my agents". "I didn't ask you that, I asked where our friend is"? "Look, you are no fool, we are playing worth some highly organized people, chances are they have your friend, but we don't know". "Well, that was some safe house". "It wasn't the house, it was where the two agents allowed you three to go, that's why they are no longer agents". I suppose that was me put in my place. So, with a heavy heart, myself and Julie were driven to the airport for our trip to Jersey, not knowing how this could end or if poor Helen was still alive. The two agents met us, Agent Stokes was a good-looking lad and appeared to be always

smiling. Phil Stanz on the other hand was about six-foot three, skinny, with a pale complexion and a dour face. I immediately christened him Mr. Dead which put a smile on Ju's face.
We jumped in their Freelander and set off for the accommodation. Mr. Dead was driving so Graham struck up a conversation. "You two must be very important, we only keep the top people safe on this island".
 "Don't you know"? "They don't tell us anything about your case, we are just here to protect you at all costs, whatever that maybe".
"Ok, we are here" Phil said.
"Now this is different Ju from the last one". It was right on the headland with nothing around it.
"Look Ju, it's even got a

swimming pool". Inside was to a high standard but we knew there was no going out and we had to make the best of this.

Time flew by and we both felt guilty lounging about by the pool every day, not knowing if Helen was ok. We must have been there for two months and if I saw another episode of friends, I think I would go mental. It was at breakfast and my turn to cook; the guys wanted a full English. I had granola and Greek yogurt. Ju always had pancakes and blueberries. "Ready lads" I shouted Ju and we sat down to eat; a few minutes had gone by when Graham said he would give her a shout. He came back and his face was ashen, "She has gone". "What do you mean,

gone"? "Gone, bloody gone".
"What have you got there"? In
his hand was a rag. "They have
taken her, its chloroform". I felt
physically sick, Julie wasn't like
Helen, she was more fragile, why
didn't they take me? My thoughts
were turning to something more
sinister. Graham and Mr. Dead
were on the phone to Clearmont,
the air was blue. I was beginning
to think I would be better off
looking after myself. That night,
I made the decision, I was going
this alone. I packed a small
backpack and, when I was sure
everybody was asleep, I climbed
out of the window.
I knew this was not ideal but look
how easily they took Helen and
Ju, there was no doubt they were
saving me to the last and I had to

know why, at the same time I had
to find my friends. I'm guessing
you think I'm nuts, but I know
what I'm doing. I sat in a coffee
shop in St Helier thinking over
my next move. "Excuse me, do
you know anywhere that has a
couple of rooms I could rent"?
The owner was English, but she
said her husband was Austrian.
"Yes, I have an annex at my
house that has just come vacant,
it's at Ouaisne Bay". "Oh, that's
great, how much"? "Well, we
also own the Smugglers Inn at
the bay so what if you did a few
shifts behind the bar and I take it
out of your wages"? "Sounds
good to me". "I'm sorry, I'm
Denise Stampfer and my husband
is Franz". I had to think quick.
"What's your name my dear"?

STUNNER FIVE

"Oh, its Trish Block". "Pleased to meet you Trish". "And you Denise". "Do you have a car? If not, I have finished for the day and can take you now". "No, I only arrived today so I've not had chance to get sorted". "No problem, I'll take you back, I'm not sure what car you want but Ellie who comes in the pub is selling her white Volkswagen Golf cabriolet". "Oh, that would be great". "Well, if you are interested, I'll take you back and will call Ellie and she will bring it over." Great I thought, if I can get mobile, I can get my hair dyed and things like that.
Ellie was waiting for us; the car was about eight years old but will do me until I can get my head straight.

STUNNER FIVE

That night I lay in bed, in some
respects feeling lucky but also
very sad. I had brought all this
misery to Helen and Julies door,
first by marrying Fabio, then
being foolish to think MI6 could
possibly protect us. I felt upset
but I had no more tears just a lust
for vengeance inside me.

The following day, I coloured my
hair black, I still had that fake
passport with me with a photo of
me with black hair so this could
come in handy.

I said I would do the next three
nights and the weekend behind
the bar. Denise was well
impressed. She was a nice person
and had been very kind to me, as
dad would have said, "Our Saron,
if you fell in a pile of cow muck
you would come up smelling of

roses". Guess he was right, but I also seemed to be a Vapona strip for disasters. The pub was lovely, all oak beams and stone flag floors and it had some nice regulars, one in particular who took a shine to me.

Prescott Graham, I asked him if it should be Graham Prescott? He said no, he could trace his family back to the early fourteen hundreds. He was a nice guy, a bit flash but we all have some dodgy traits. He was six foot tall with jet black hair and a toned physique. He started coming in every night I worked, and we slowly got to know each other, he told me his family owned five top hotels on Jersey and two in Guernsey. He corrected himself and said it had been a family business but there was just his mum and him now and she was having twenty-four-hour care in a specialist dementia hospital. After about three weeks, he asked if, next time I wasn't working, would I like to go for a meal with him. What the hell I thought, I can't just sit in my room night after night worrying about Ju and Helen.

It was a Thursday night and I waited by the steps to the Smugglers when a Bentley Arnage Cabriolet pulled up, it was a beautiful Graphite Grey colour. "Hop in Saron" he said with a big cheesy smile. "Where are we going"? "The Lobster Pot on the Five Mile Road, sorry, it's not called that now, it's called

Frammpe". The restaurant didn't look much on the outside other than the view of course but inside, talk about lavish, and the staff were falling over themselves looking after us, Prescott must have been a big hitter on the island.

It was an excellent menu, and I was relieved to see they had good vegan and vegetarian options. I went for the filo cheese parcels with a plum dip followed by an unusual vegetarian lasagna which had like a crumble top that would normally have been on an apple crumble, but it was divine. We never stopped talking, it was mainly about Prescott because I didn't want to let anything out of the bag about me and at the minute it suited me to let him

think I was just a summer
worker, there was no pressure
that way. He brought me back to
the annex and was a complete
gentleman. From my side, I still
wasn't over Fabio. The months
went by, but thoughts of my
friends never dimmed. It was
early August, and I was getting
ready for work. An appeal came
up on Sky News, there was
Clearmont, Mr. Dead and
Graham Stokes sat at what
looked like a news conference.
"This is an appeal to the general
public of Jersey in the Channel
Islands. Three young girls we
believe are in grave danger, they
are Julie Bentley" and he showed
a picture of Ju then Helen then
me, then he said Ju and Helen
had been taken from a safe house

and whilst my disappearance was
similar, he believed I was on the
run and possibly still in danger.
"If you are watching this Saron,
you need to come back into our
custody, there have been
developments".
Now what? I thought. Luckily, I
had kept my black hair, but it
didn't stop some locals picking
up on the resemblance that night.
I just brushed it off but deep
down this had put me back in
danger and maybe I should go
back to MI6.
I made my decision; it was
getting to the end of the season,
so I told Denise I had business at
home to sort out. Denise was fine
so the following day I headed for
London and MI6. Gavin
Clearmont was pleased to see me

although the opening dialogue
was a bit tense. "Saron what the
hell are you playing at"? "What
am I playing at? My two best
friends are taken, and you lot
could not stop it happening"?
"We have a lead on your friends,
they are alive and are being held
in a house in Austria, CS have a
lot of support there, it's
something to do with the war and
Hitler annexing his homeland.
Many jews thought they were
safe, hence CS have huge support
because of the atrocities handed
out to the Austrian Jews. I
believe we have one shot at this,
it's you they want, the reason
they have your friends is because
they knew that would flush you
out. If you want this to be over
and you and your friends live,

then you have this one chance.
You will be given intense
training by MI6. You will get a
false passport and you will
infiltrate CS". "What are you,
bloody mental? If I do this, what
is it all for"? "We believe they
have some dirt on their Prime
Minister and that is why they are
allowed to do what they do so
your job is to find out what it is
for MI6, and we will use this to
trade yours, Julie and Helen's
lives then this goes away".
"Ok, when do I start"? "Just a
moment, send in Agent Fearn".
This guy came in, he was about
six foot tall, very athletic and had
a Yorkshire accent. "Where are
you from"? I asked. "Originally,
I was born just outside Heathcliff
in a tiny hamlet called Diddle Me

STUNNER FIVE

Dale". "Really? I'm from
Heathcliff, I had a friend in
Diddle Me Dale". "What was her
name"? "Alison Fearn". "That's
my sister". "Wow, small world
so what's your name"? "Paul".
"Well, nice to meet you, how is
Alison"? "You don't know"?
"Know what"? "She was killed in
a car accident about nine months
ago, some scumbag high on
drugs hit her head on she had no
chance". "Oh, I am sorry Paul,
we sort of lost touch". "That's
ok, we all have busy lives, don't
beat yourself up about it".
Paul was my mentor, I had six
months of training and at the end
I felt like superwoman. I had got
to know Paul really well and
assumed he was coming to
Austria with me, but I got that

very wrong. I was to be on my own. MI6 could not allow CS to know MI6 were involved, they basically told me that if they rumbled me, I was on my own. Charming I thought as I boarded the plane for Austria with my new identity and a Glock pistol in my hand luggage which I was told would not be a problem at security. It wasn't, I breezed through and picked up a car at the airport for the drive to Kufstein, apparently that's where Ju and Helen were and the head man at CS who was my target. They had told me that Rudy Gasty, the head man, liked the girls and frequented a bar called Freche Bar which, roughly translated, meant Naughty Bar. I dressed up the first night, I had

been trained on what Rudy liked
etc. and luckily, he liked slim
brunettes, so that was a start
seeing as my hair was still dyed
dark. Attracting his attention
wasn't going to be a problem for
me, I sat at the bar showing just
enough leg to arouse his interest.
He came in the bar with two
other guys, I was guessing they
were his minders. Rudy was
about five foot ten with a goatee
beard, steely brown eyes and I
would say he was in his early
fifties. The place lit up when he
walked in, many of the girls
throwing themselves at him. He
loved it, he kept ordering
champagne. Eventually he came
over. "Your name, what is your
name"? he said in abrupt manner.
I never answered. He turned to

the barman, "Give the lady champagne". "I'm fine thank you, I am leaving now", I got up to go and he grabbed my arm. "Next time I see you, we drink together". I just smiled and left, knowing he was on the hook. The hotel was two blocks away and I kept wondering where my friends were, but I had to play it like MI6 said or we would never be free from CS. I left it two nights then went in the bar again, Rudy Gasty was sat playing the king in the corner with girls hanging on his every word, but he noticed me. I wore a green dress, very short showing my legs, with a slightly plunging neckline. Like dad used to say, don't put it in the shop window if it isn't for sale. After an hour of him

playing Mr. Cool, he came over.
"So, how are you? You never
told me your name". I nearly said
Saron then remembered my new
identity. "Oh, its Athena
Golden". "Very nice to meet you
Athena Golden" he said grabbing
my hand and lightly kissing it. I
knew what I had to do and being
with this monster was part of the
remit if we were ever going to be
free.

 I must admit, this man made my
flesh crawl knowing the atrocities
he was carrying out in the name
of the Jewish people. That all
aside, from that night I started to
get close to him and slowly but
surely, he opened up to me. Yes,
there were bad bits like having to
sleep with this specimen. It took
almost three months for him to

tell me about CS and he truly believed in what he did. With a bit of bravado, I managed to get him talking about Julie and Helen, he said one was quiet and one was feisty which would have been Helen. He said he had come close to putting a gun to her head, but her friend had information he needed. Little did he know that it was me!

I decide to try and find out about the Prime Minister. Surprisingly, he sang like a canary. He spoke openly about Mosha Desney, he said he had been in power for fourteen years and had allowed CS to grow unrestricted but there was a price to pay for his loyalty. "In the early years, they found out that Mosha had been a Kapo in Sobibor. He did it to save his own skin, even putting his grandfather, grandmother and his brother to the gas chambers. His crime would never have been found until, in nineteen eighty-four, a journalist was snigging about, and he ordered us to get rid of the leech as he termed him. We did it on the understanding that we would operate freely. Before we killed the journalist, we took all his information. I carry it about with me and never let it out of my sight Athena".

I had noticed he always had a black leather man bag on him. If it was in there this wasn't going to be easy for me to get the information for MI6.

I had one chance at this. I called Clearmont and told him what I had been told. "We need the evidence Saron". "I understand but what if they kill Julie and Helen once I take it because they no longer have a use"? "Once you have the information and are safely on a flight, we will contact CS Rudy Gasty and tell him the deal is Helen and Julie alive and his wolves called off you. He won't want to jeopardise CS so it will be fine Saron, good luck and well done".

It was alright for Clearmont I thought, but I still have to somehow drug Rudy then get past his to bodyguards that stood at his bedroom door and then get on a plane. Well, if anyone can pull it off Saron can I thought. I spent time in my room concocting a sleeping agent that would give me about ten hours grace. Once he was asleep, I just rubbed it on his lips and boom, he is a distant memory or is that a distant nightmare? Deep down I wanted to kill him for what he had done to Fabio and the girls, but I had to play to the rules. It was two nights later when he arranged dinner, so I booked a flight out of Austria. First, I had to find where he was holding Julie and Helen in case it all went wrong. Over dinner he was laughing and joking, he mentioned a few times a bakery and the girls. Now I had at least a clue where they were. Back at the room I felt physically sick making love with this man, he was just so horrible. I kept saying to myself this is the last time. Eventually it was over, and he fell asleep, I got the sleeping drug out of my handbag then placed a few drops on his lips, he murmured, and I thought at one point he was going to wake up as I fumbled in his black leather man-bag. I got all the information. I quickly showered then I called the two guards in saying I thought Rudy was unwell. I shot them both with my gun equipped with a silencer, one slumped on the bed and the other lay on the floor.

I went down the fire exit escalator so that I didn't raise suspicion with the night porter. I jumped in a taxi and was soon on a plane home, just before we took off, I called Clearmont. "Ok, come in tomorrow for a de-brief and well done. Agent Fearn will pick you up at Heathrow and bring you here". "Ok, thanks" I said and settled down to have a quick sleep before London. I arrived at Heathrow to typical English weather, it was cold and wet. I breezed through and Paul was waiting for me in the concourse. "Hurry Saron, we might miss the rush hour traffic, in and out of London". Paul had a black Jaguar X Pace which was sooo comfortable after the plane journey and I fell asleep. When I woke, I was in a wooden hut with a gun at my head. "What the hell is going on"? "Do you think we are stupid? You are dealing with CS". My mind was racing, when I put my bag in the boot of Paul's vehicle, I hid the papers under the boot carpet, just in case.

STUNNER FIVE

"Your agent is behind you". I could just turn enough to see Paul being interrogated and tortured. "So, Tricky Miss Saron, Rudy wants his documents back". "What documents"? Paul let out a scream. "Why are you hurting him? He was just a driver". "We hurt him until you give back the documents". I had clocked there were three men including the torturer. "Ok, let him go and I will take you to them, I'm not as stupid as you think". "He is going nowhere, give me the documents". "You will have to take me back to Heathrow". "Ok, untie him". His next action shook me, he calmly wandered over to Paul and shot him, he fell forward. These people were ruthless, I had to get this information to Clearmont. I had noticed that only one of them had a gun, so he was the one to take out as they frog marched me to their van. I spun around and disarmed the guy then shot the other two, after a bit of a struggle I managed to shoot the other one. Lara Croft would have been proud of me. I then ran to the vehicle and drove to London. I phoned Clearmont on the way and told him what had happened. "Phone CS and tell them you have all this information on their Prime Minister and if the girls are not released in the next two hours and we have pictures of them boarding the plane to the UK then we go public to the tabloids".

STUNNER FIVE

By now I was at MI6 and the
pictures came through of Ju and
Helen boarding the plane. I was
in the office of Gavin Clearmont
when the call came through from
CS saying that, as long as MI6
never repeated what they knew
then Julie, Helen and myself
would not be harmed. I can't tell
you the relief I felt but sadness
that a good man, Agent Paul
Fearn, had lost his life.
"I'm going to pick them up
Gavin, please don't contact me
again, I don't need this in my
life, I just want to enjoy it".
Clearmont just smiled and let me
out of his office. The drive to
Heathrow was one I had dreamt
of for so long. The girls were
ecstatic to have been released and
over a bottle or two of red wine

and a lasagna with salad I told
them what had happened.

Chapter 5

The following day we set off to
see the café bistro, it was almost
finished and looked amazing.
Hopefully, I can keep out of
scrapes and not involve the girls
which I felt terrible about.
We were all looking forward to
the new season and our shiny
new café bistro. We had changed
our mind's so many times on the
name but, over a few bottles one

night in Fowey, we heard the
Thin Lizzy song, The Boys are
Back in Town, so we decided on
The Girls are Back in Town, a bit
cheesy I know but after what we
had been through it seemed a
good idea.
Christmas came to Polruan, and
we decided we would spend
Christmas Eve at a new bar
called The Beaver in Fowey that
way we weren't far from home.
You can imagine it was packed,
they had carol singers from Truro
Cathedral at 9.30pm and it even
snowed a bit. Ju was getting
some attention from a lad that
had the chippy up the road, they
called him quick draw Magraw
for some reason. Ju said he had
told her that, when he was little,
he always wore a cowboy hat and

wore play guns on a holster belt.
It made me laugh and you can
imagine Helen's comment to that
one. I just wanted Ju to be happy,
she had been through so much
and she was so kind to everybody
she deserved some happiness and
if quick draw was the solution so
be it. I was chatted up a few
times but Fabio was still in my
heart so I couldn't strike a
relationship up with anybody just
yet. We had a lovely Christmas
day, we all worked on the
Christmas dinner, and it was
fabulous. Christmas night Ju
went to meet quick draws parents
so me and Helen played scrabble,
which of course she was just
brilliant at, even though we
downed three bottles of Malbec,

but it hardly seemed to affect
Hell's Bell's.
The next few weeks were spent
interviewing, Ju did the waitress'
and cleaning staff, Helen did bar
people and accommodation
which left me with catering. I set
on a kitchen porter, Maurice, he
was about fifty-six and a nice
guy, he had been high up in
Anglia Water but got made
redundant. Him and his wife
loved Cornwall, so they sort of
retired here and the kitchen job
was just pin money for him.
I took on Alan as the second
chef, he had worked at numerous
holiday locations, Torquay,
Whitby etc. and had a good CV.
The one I struggled with because
it's so important was the head
chef. I had interviewed about

eight, some wanted too much
money, others you could see
were just p**s heads.
I had arranged to go back and see
Denise and tell her the whole
truth, I felt I owed her that so she
might be able to point me in the
right direction. I asked the girls if
they wanted to come but they still
hadn't got their staff sorted and
seeing it was only a week until
we opened, they decided not to
bother.
I was kind of looking forward to
seeing Denise and some of the
locals but was a bit apprehensive.
I really don't like liars but, in that
instance, I had no choice. I
arrived in Jersey and got a little
Fiat 500 C hire car and drove to
the Biarritz where I had booked
in for the week. It was a lovely

hotel, it felt really comfortable. The following day I drove into St Helier and Denise's coffee shop. At first, she didn't recognize me with my hair back to blonde. When she did, she flung her arms around me. "I wondered if we would ever see you again". There weren't many in, so she got us a coffee and a piece of homemade ginger cake, and we sat and talked. Well, I talked, poor Denise could hardly believe what I was telling her. "So, when I met you, it was because you were on the run from this CS group and MI6 Saron"? "Yes, I know it all sounds incredible". "It does feel weird calling you Saron not Trish love. So, your friends are back safe, and sound and you are of course". I never told her about the killings, she was in shock enough. "Hey, wait until I tell Franz with him being Austrian, he will know the places you talked about. Where are you staying and for how long"? "I'm stopping at the Biarritz just for a week, I needed to come and tell you the truth Denise". "You could have stopped with me and Franz love" and she hugged me again.

"Well, we must do some things together while you are here". "Definitely, that would be fun. Do you still get the same locals in at the Smugglers"? "Oh yes love, old Jack is always talking about you. Do you remember Dick and Margo? She was always a bit snooty". "Oh yeah, I remember her". "Well, a bit of gossip for you, she left Dick, they had been married forty years and she is now with Larry the car salesman"! "Not Larry the letch Denise"? "The very same love". "Blimey, some peoples taste hey? What about Susie the waitress"? "She went travelling at the end of the season, I had a letter from her, she is doing the cruise ships now.

Do you fancy going to the Butterfly farm at Greve De Lecq tomorrow then have lunch at the Windmill". "Oh, that would be lovely Denise". "Ok, I'll pick you up about 12.15 pm tomorrow, Saron. Are you going to the Smugglers tonight"? "No, I thought I might call in tomorrow". "Ok love, I will see you tomorrow then".

STUNNER FIVE

I told Denise I wouldn't be going
tonight as I had a few things
nagging at me so needed time to
think. I showered and ordered a
salad from room service then I
got a pen and paper and made
two columns, I was trying to
decide what was nagging at me.
First, I wrote, Why kidnap Ju and
Helen and leave me to the last,
what was the gain?
 I then wrote, MI6 involvement,
Gavin Clearmont. Then I wrote,
Pictures of Clearmont. It was
starting to come clear, well, at
least I thought it was, I began to
realise this was a stitch up.
Initially Clearmont needed me
for the information, which I gave
him, he wasn't stupid he knew I
would have copies of the pictures
of him, and he couldn't allow

that. I now had two enemies and CS were the lesser, Clearmont was my biggest threat. But how do I handle the head of MI6 and all his resources?

The following day, Denise picked me up and we headed for the Butterfly Farm. We were having such a good time, the blue butterflies took a shine to me in the enclosure, they were all over me, it was then that I got a shock, I saw Paul Fearn through the haze of butterflies surrounding me but by the time I got out there was no sign of him. Was I mistaken? Paul was dead.

"You alright love? I've never seen so many butterflies around one person in all the years of coming here". "Let's go and have lunch Denise". They sat at a table in the window with Saron insisting. "Denise, I think I'm paranoid, I saw a guy from MI6 at the butterfly farm". "Maybe he was on holiday love, we are a holiday island after all". "You don't understand, he was shot dead in front of me". I suddenly realised this was too much information for poor Denise to comprehend. "You must be mistaken love". "Yeah, you're right. Ok what do you recommend from the menu"? "Well love, the fish pie au gratin, they do a lovely cheese dumpling with Jersey royals and feta salad". "That sounds great I'm going to have that, Denise". She wasn't wrong, it really was nice. I told Denise about Cornwall, and the girls are back in town bistro.

STUNNER FIVE

It felt like I had a great new friend in Denise, and we had a lovely day. That night I was going to the Smugglers to meet some old friends. I showered at the Biarritz then set off for the Smugglers still a bit confused about seeing who I thought was Paul Fearn. Looking back, once I gave Clearmont the information on CS it did seem a bit easier than I expected but I was beginning to doubt Clearmont. Anyway, I need to forget that and enjoy the few days away. I walked into a big cheer which was lovely. Old Sid was adamant he was buying me a drink. Larry the Letch and Margo collared me. "Blonde suits you don't it Larry"? "Yes, a sexy blonde bombshell". Typical Larry, with

that Margo shot me a dirty look.
Nothing changes I thought.
I had a lovely night; everybody
was so nice to me. I stopped at
Denise's due to the alcohol
consumption. The short break
was soon over, and I had decided
to fly to London to confront
Clearmont. I'm sure he had been
behind some of the weird things.
I arranged to meet him at a bar in
Carnaby Street which I knew
would be packed with tourists
because I was convinced, he
wanted me dead so the pictures
would not surface.
I arrived at 2.00pm and I could
see Clearmont in the window.
Again, suspicion took over, why
sit in the window? I got to his
table, and he had already ordered
a bottle of red wine and two

glasses. "Saron, looking Stunning as usual" and he kissed my hand. "Why the secrecy"? "Bloody hell Gavin, that's a case of the pot calling the kettle". "So, what is our little meaning about"? "Well, first of all, Paul Fearn, I saw him in Jersey, but I thought he was dead". "So how could you have seen him"? "I know how this works Gavin, our freedom, when it happened, all seemed too easy the more I thought about it then, seeing Agent Fearn at the Butterfly Farm confirmed it". I luckily bent down to pick up a little boy's football that he dropped when a shot rang out, the glass shattered, and a bullet stuck in the wood of the seat exactly where my head would have been.

"Come Saron, quickly, before the police arrive". There was mayhem in the bar and to be honest, I was really shaken up. Once we were far enough away Clearmont told me that the deal made with CS was for Julie and Helen, but they could not get the ok to drop me as I had been married to, what they called, a Nazi. Clearmont said he was concerned but he hadn't sent an agent to Jersey. I wasn't sure if this was BS and that he was more concerned with the pictures I have of him and I was sure he wanted me dead more than CS. "So why can't you protect me? You know who these people are, and I gave you information". He just did a silly smirk, and I knew then he was driving this but how did I stop it? I had to quickly get my thinking head on. I decided to play along with him, as dad used to say, "keep your friends close and your enemies closer". Never a truer word said with my current predicament. "Gavin, I'm going back to my hotel, with it being Friday do you fancy a weekend away"? I knew he would not be able to resist. "Where do you fancy"? "Do you know, I haven't been to Flamborough Head since I was a little girl so let's do that". "Great, I will pick you up at 7.00 am in the morning". My plan was to push him off Flamborough Head. Little did I know what was in store for me that night as I fell asleep in the comfy hotel bed. I had fallen asleep when suddenly I felt pressure on my mouth. My eyes opened in pure panic to see Agent Paul Fearn stood over signaling for me to be quiet. "It was you I saw at the Butterfly farm in Jersey, I'm guessing you are here to do Clearmont's dirty work". "No, I am here to help you. Make us a coffee and I will explain". Now I am confused Paul". We sat on the bed and Paul started to unravel what he knew.

"Clearmont is in over his head, he knew I was aware, I fully expected him to have me killed hence, what you saw was a set up. I had arranged it simply for the fact that I knew you were being set up to be murdered. I can't tell you all the details, but this goes right to the top. My suggestion would be to go back to Cornwall, and I will meet you there hopefully then this mess can be sorted". Paul looked at me and we both knew what we were thinking, he tenderly kissed me then left, I could tell he wasn't sure if that was what I wanted!! I decided to get back to Cornwall with Ju and Helen in my comfort zone. I was intrigued with what Paul had told me but felt better knowing I had somebody batting for me. Like I expected, the girls were over the moon to see me and over a few glasses of Prosecco in the King of Prussia in Fowey I told them what had happened. They were gob-smacked, my life, as Helen put it, was in permanent James Bond mode which made me laugh, typical Hells Bells. Ju said her fling with the latest bloke had run its course and they were now busy with The Girls are Back in Town. They said the season had really taken off and the accommodation was always fully booked.

Chapter 6

It was almost a month before Paul Fearn came to see me. We met at the coffee shop in Polruan, he was quite a shy guy and I think a little bit embarrassed about the kiss in the hotel room. He said what he had to tell me was mega sensitive and I could not repeat it to anyone. Of course, I said I wouldn't. He then started to tell me the story.

STUNNER FIVE

They said for many years Fabio
had been a double agent, but his
leaning was always to MI6 and
the work he did by being a
double agent saved so many
agents lives across the globe, it
more than outweighed the
situation. Paul said him and
Fabio had been friends since he
was recruited from the Special
Boat Services, and he said Fabio
took him under his wing. He told
me, after about three years, that
he was going to retire but then he
told me about CS and said they
would hunt him and his wife
down. Paul said he didn't want to
upset me, but Fabio had told him
his wife was the world to him, so
he planned to buy a boat and
travel the seas out of harm's way.
"He was devastated but I told

him he had to still do it and we
joked he might meet a pretty
maiden. It was a massive surprise
when he met you, it gave him a
new lease. He was so happy". "If
you were such a big friend, how
come you weren't at our
wedding, and he never spoke of
you"? "I had already started
finding things out about
Clearmont so couldn't make it
and agents never discuss other
agents in the field Saron". "I
want to believe you Paul but
there is so much intrigue and
dishonesty its difficult. Let's go
back to my place and have a
coffee and we can talk more
privately".

When Paul started to unravel the
full meaning of why I was in this
pickle I was shocked. Clearmont

had done some dodgy dealing
with not just CS but also the
Russian Secret Service and
Mossad. Fabio, before he retired,
had discovered what had been
going on. "I told him to let
sleeping dogs lie. He had done
his bit and should just retire".
Although Fabio had agreed Paul
said he couldn't help himself and
told Clearmont what an asshole
he was. "Clearmont wasn't going
to take that, and I am pretty sure
he tried to kill him but then,
when Fabio married you, he had
another problem, he didn't know
what Fabio had told you, so you
had to be disposed of. From my
side, he knew me, and Fabio
were friends so again assumed I
may know something, so I was
on his, dispose of at any costs,

list. To be honest I was quite shocked, Clearmont was a powerful man, he knew I would have those pictures of him, he also knew I had duped him with CS.

"Paul, I have thought about going to the newspapers with my story, that way it would be difficult to kill me". "Don't be so sure, looking through the ages, and I am not naming names, but they have died and whilst conspiracist may comment, nothing is ever proven. Paul was right, that's a daft idea. Did I revert to killing Clearmont? Now Paul was on my side he would get dragged into it if I did.

That night Paul stayed; we made love, he was a gentle lover, more concerned about me than himself which was nice. I know what you are thinking but I must move on from Fabio, I really do, or I will go stir crazy. The following morning, I could tell Paul wasn't a player, he was very attentive towards me and whilst I liked it, I wasn't sure if I could handle that attention all the time.

Over breakfast, we discussed the next move. Paul was adamant that he alone must sort the situation, he didn't want me involved.

He told me that he was divorced, he said the job took its toll on the marriage, Connie and him had met when they were sixteen and he had two children, Simon who he said was eleven and Jasmin who was nine. He said Connie had been to a school reunion and

met a lad from her year who was
a car salesman, and she went off
with him, she told Paul that if
ever engaged with the guy he
would never see his kids again.
He seemed a nice guy and
somewhat vulnerable, I just
hoped he was hanging his hopes
on me!!

We parted that day and then I
heard nothing, it was kind of
weird, I was forever weighing
people up, always on the alert
that at any time my life could be
over. The season finished and me
and the girls decided to go on
holiday. Ju wanted a cruise. I
wasn't a cruise type of person,
but Helen said she was fine with
it, so we booked it. We were to
sail from Southampton to the

STUNNER FIVE

Eastern Caribbean in three days' time, so shopping was the order of the day. We took a train to London and stayed overnight. What a shopping spree it was. I bought quite a revealing red swimsuit like they used to wear in Baywatch but mine was a bit more revealing. Helen said now my hair had grown she thought I looked equally as good as Pamela Anderson, mind, we were on our third bottle of wine over dinner at the Ivy!

We were so excited. Helen treated herself to some new Gucci sunglasses as did Ju. "We will knock them for dead" Hells Bells confidently predicted. I was sure she was correct in her thoughts.

STUNNER FIVE

A couple of days later we arrived at Southampton, the boat was huge with seven dining areas all themed differently, Chinese, American, British, French, Italian, Japanese and South American. We chose the endless drink package; the first stop was going to be the Bahamas. The entertainment was good, first they had The Bootleg Beatles who were excellent and supporting was Rick Astley. We danced and danced, my poor feet were killing me, but I kept my stilettos on like a good trooper. We staggered back to our rooms having had a brilliant night. We said we would meet for breakfast the next day.

STUNNER FIVE

Of course, Hells Bells was there before anyone, no hang over for her and she was tucking into poached egg on toast when I got there. Ju finally arrived looking dreadful. "I feel so rough, my mouth feels like the bottom of a budgie cage". Me and Helen were laughing so much it was a wonder we didn't have an accident. "Ju, you are so funny with your sayings. Poor Ju was oblivious and left soon after to go to a darkened room. We finally arrived in Nassau at Prince George dock, the weather was fabulous, we were told to be back for 6.00 pm that night. That was the only thing that was regimented but I guess they had a schedule to run too. We got a taxi into Nassau and paid him extra so he would take us back that night. Julie was paranoid about being late.

For some reason, Helen wanted to go to the World Bimini Casino, she said she felt lucky so dragged us along with her. What a choice, it was just fabulous, we had a couple of hours playing roulette. Ju won the equivalent of three hundred and eighty pounds, Helen won two hundred and ninety and I won ninety-eight pounds, I guess that was because I was more reckless than them. No change there then I can hear you say! Next, we went to Biminis Fisherman's village for shopping and lunch. Ju bought a beautiful emerald brooch then we had lunch at Salty Dogs. The

food was to die for, the
camembert and chili pasta was
delicious, and the girls tucked
into the local fish. They say time
flies when you're having fun and
it was soon 4.30 pm so we
decided to head back. There was
a medium on tonight and we
really wanted to see her. That
night, surprisingly, the theatre
wasn't packed to see Mary
Forest. She was well known but I
guess some people just don't like
that sort of thing. Mary was soon
into her show and asked if
anybody in the audience whose
friend or maybe father was
interested in cars. Helen nudged
me, "Your dad was mate". "I
know but let's see how it
evolves". Two people put their
hand up. "This gentleman seems

agitated; he is saying it's his daughter he wants to speak to". One was a man who had stood up, so he sat down. "What's your name dear"? she said. "It's Karen". "I have Karen here, what do you want to say to her? I'm afraid he has gone quiet. He is making a sign with his hand. Is that an S" she said to the spirit. "He is nodding at me". "Saron, the message is for you". I stood up. "Who are you dear"? "My name is Saron and my father loved cars". "He seems happier now. Do you want to ask him anything"? "Yes, is mum ok"? "Yes, he is nodding. He is saying everything you see isn't everything you, see? Does that mean anything to you? Oh, dear, I am sorry, he has gone". There

were no more messages for me or
Ju and Helen although we all
wondered what dad had meant, if
indeed it was dad I thought!!

Next, we were sailing to
Charlotte Amalia, St Thomas. Ju
had one of those little travel
books and the place looked
fabulous, we would be staying
two nights at the Empress Amalia
so would have time to explore
and get the tan topped up. I
hadn't noticed that I had
inadvertently put my mobile on
silent and had twenty missed
calls and messages from Paul
Fearn. I have to say I was
worried but didn't tell the others,
I didn't want them to worry so I
waited until I was in my room.

"Paul, its Saron, are you, ok"?
"Where the hell are you"? He
sounded extremely worried. "I'm
on a cruise". "Where"? "The
Caribbean". "Are you anywhere
near Puerto Rico"? "We go there
next Paul". "Right, I will contact
you in the next couple of days"
and he hung up. Something isn't
right, when I said the Caribbean,
he said was I near Puerto Rico,
now I might be paranoid but to
pick the next place we were
going to seemed odd. I didn't tell
the girls, no point in ruining their
holiday.

The more I thought about it the
more stupid I was being, if Paul
was working for Clearmont he
could have killed me in the hotel
room that night. On our last night

before Puerto Rico the girls were
dancing, I was sat with my
thoughts. I suddenly remembered
something Fabio told me on our
wedding night, he gave me a key
but said I was never to open the
safety deposit box unless I was in
grave danger. I had the key sewn
into a Mulberry scarf which I
took everywhere with me.

It was decision time, did I take
my chance with agent Fearn or
cut short the holiday and go and
look what was in the safety
deposit box? My decision making
as you know is not one of my
best traits, so I flipped a coin.
Heads its Puerto Rico and a
liaison with agent Fearn or tails
head for London and the safety

deposit box. I sat on my bed and flipped the coin, it seemed to take an age before finally hitting the floor then rolling, it stopped heads up, Puerto Rico it is then, I just hope I don't live to regret it!!

The following day the girls were asking if I was ok as I wasn't my party animal self. I told them that Paul Fearn was going to meet with me, and I gave Ju the scarf. "Please keep it safe and don't give the key to anyone" and I explained what Fabio had said. Whilst she was shocked and concerned Ju trusted me. I said she wasn't even to tell Helen. Ju understood. We decided to do an excursion to old San Juan, there was so much history, and the place had a carnival atmosphere,

the people were so lovely. We
danced and drank copious
amounts of Pina Colada,
apparently it was invented there
in 1978. Helen got into a
drinking competition with
Wilfred, a local guy, but I'm
afraid he was no match for our
Hells Bells. I so wanted this thing
hanging over me to go away and
just live a normal life, I was sick
of looking over my shoulder
every day

We had a lovely night, when I
got back to the hotel Fearn rang
me. "Saron, it's Paul" I always
think some people are weird, if
they are in your contacts it comes
up on your phone who it is!! "In
the town there is a monument of
a soldier in the square. I will be

at the coffee shop; it's called Hendricks Coffee Lounge". "Ok, what time"? "9.30 am". "Ok Paul, see you then". The phone went dead, and I was beginning to think maybe I had made a mistake.

I arrived promptly, Fearn looked nervous. Over a coffee he told me that CA were no longer after my friends or me, but that Clearmont was after me, he said that Clearmont said I would know too much from Fabio and that was why he was also after him. He said he had booked flights to London, and we needed to go that afternoon. It all sounded plausible. "What will we do in London Paul"? "I have a safe house just outside London in

Epping Forest, we will be safe there until I can sort Clearmont". We headed for the airport, and he told me to give him my mobile phone and he threw it away, he said they could track me. I was pleased I had confided in Ju.

Paul got us a taxi when we landed, and we headed to Epping Forest. We must have been about in the centre of the forest, there was a small log cabin. He paid the taxi driver and once we got inside, Fearn pulled out a gun and made me sit in a chair and he tied my hands and feet. "What the hell is going on Paul"? "Ok, it is time we stopped these silly games. Fabio had a deposit box didn't he"? "What the hell are you talking about"? Fearn then slapped me hard. "I want the key Saron, give it me and I will let you live, your choice". I knew now he had every intention of killing me once he had extracted from me where the key was. "A few days of no food will loosen your tongue" he said, disappearing into the kitchen. I had to stay calm, I hadn't expected this. How was I going to get out of this mess?

On the third day there was a knock at the door, maybe this was my chance. Fearn put tape over my mouth and threatened me if I made a sound. Somebody knocked at the door again, Fearn opened the door. I heard a voice say, "Good afternoon, I'm Craig Brown from the estate agents, we like to periodically check on our rental properties". "I can assure you everything is fine". "I'll just take a quick look" and he barged past Fearn. His face was a picture when he was confronted with a woman tied to a chair, then Fearn shot him in the back of the head, and he dropped to the floor. "What have you done Paul"? "Shut up and tell me where the key is". This was getting worse by the minute, Fearn slapped me again, he was now mega agitated. "Fabio never told me anything about his work". "You are lying, I need to get into that safety deposit box before Clearmont". "What is so special that you would kill for it"? I said with blood from the leasing agents head now a sticky mess near my

feet. "You have one more day
and if you don't tell me then I
have no choice but to torture
you". With that he disappeared
upstairs. I was hungry, thirsty
and annoyed, I had allowed
myself to be tricked, how stupid
of me. I knew I needed a game
plan; this man was desperate and
there was no way he was going to
let me live if I gave up the key.
By nightfall I could hear Fearn
snoring upstairs, this was my
chance, I dragged me and the
chair towards a knife on the side
trying desperately not to make
too much noise. When I was
little, I had a party trick where I
could make my wrist limp. I tried
it and it worked, my hands were
free, so I cut my legs free. Now
to get out of here. I unbolted the

kitchen door and just ran. I had
run about a mile when I came
across a family, I made up a story
that my boyfriend was violent in
drink, so I walked out on him.
They said they were leaving
today, and did I need a lift
anywhere? They were from
Bristol, so I said the train station
in Bristol please. I wasn't sure if
I was doing the right thing and
would have to wait for Ju to get
back to get the all-important key,
then maybe I can unravel this
mess. My thinking was Paul
Fearn would not expect me to go
to Cornwall. I backed my gut
feeling that he thought I would
head for London. I bought a pay
as you go phone and would
borrow money off Ju. If I used a
cash machine, they would find

me easily. The next week and a
half I spent changing my
appearance like I seemed to have
to do regularly. I must admit I
was a nervous wreck by the time
Ju and Helen got back. Needless
to say, my two best friends were
pleased to see me and I them.
Helen said she was having an
early night which gave me the
opportunity to tell Julie
everything. It wasn't that I didn't
want to tell Helen but why drag
her in to this mess? I unpicked
the scarf and got the key then I
told Ju I would be gone when she
got back the following night and
to wish me luck. We both had a
few tears because this time I
really wasn't sure how this could
end and the vibe we both felt
wasn't a good one. I left for

STUNNER FIVE

London and the Terminus
Goldstream Bank on Oxford
Street.

Chapter 7

It was a fabulous building, I was
so nervous, my mouth felt dry.
Whatever was in the box must
have been so important to
Clearmont and Fearn that they
would kill for it. Well, I was
about to find out. I was taken

down into the bank vaults and a room with at least two hundred and fifty boxes. My key was number fifty-eight. I walked over to the security box, my whole body filled with anxiety. I felt physically sick as I opened the box, inside was a larger key and a handwritten letter,

"My beautiful Saron

Let me say first that I am so sorry you have been dragged into this. I have no choice with not being here to protect you so this is the only way I could think of saving you. You will see in my will that I left everything to you. Please enjoy every moment of your life sweetheart. There is two hundred thousand pounds in this box and a lot more in my estate. You will need to contact Mitchell and Spear in Newcastle, my solicitors, who know you will arrive one day. When I say one day it's because MI6, or should I say Fearn and Clearmont will, track calls etc.

This is my plan, take the money and the key and fly to Sardinia, there is a village called Agremont, there you will find a bar called Micky's Bar, it is a front for an organisation called Agent Son's, they will look after you, I won't go into too much detail, Leonardo is the man you need to contact when you show him the key he will accept you. You will be safe with them, but I have no doubt MI6 will come calling and the key to the second box is your last resort bargaining chip,

Goodbye my darling wife, please find somebody who will love you as much as I did.

Fabio xx"

I sat and cried, why did I have to lose such a beautiful caring man, why me? Awash with self- pity I booked a flight the next day to Sardinia. I bought another pay as you go phone, my only worry was if they were checking airports, so I took a flight from Luton, I figured they were more likely to be checking Heathrow and Stansted.

STUNNER FIVE

It was really hot when I arrived and jumped into a taxi to take me to Agremont and Micky's Bar. The bar looked like something out of the movie Goodfellows, I fully expected one of the characters to come talking to me. A swarthy looking bloke served me a margarita. "Are you on holiday"? he asked. "Sort of. I am looking for Leonardo". On hearing that name he disappeared down the other end of the bar pretending to clean glasses. I sat for a good twenty minutes, with my drink finished I was contemplating my next move when I felt a tap on my shoulder.

I spun around and the most gorgeous man I think I had ever encountered was standing there.

STUNNER FIVE

He uttered the words "Are you looking for me"? "Are you Leonardo"? "Who is asking"? "I'm Saron, I was married to Fabio". He instantly hugged me, I felt my legs go like jelly, he was gorgeous. "Two margaritas" he shouted to the barman who came scurrying back to us. Whoever this guy was, he was feared, of that there was no doubt. "So, you are the beautiful Saron, the wife of my dear friend Fabio, sadly no longer with us". He spoke in that sexy Italian voice. His eyes were incredible, and his body was amazing. I kept thinking he was the most handsome man I had ever seen, he seemed perfect, He ordered another margarita and then, to my surprise, a lady came from the back with a little girl who I thought would have been about three. "Saron, meet my family, Oskala my wife and our little girl, Sophia".

With my bubble burst I said hello and they joined us. She was a lovely lady, but her English wasn't very good, so they kept breaking into their native Italian. Eventually Oskala said she had to take Sophia to bed, so she said goodnight. Don't think bad of me but Leonardo was such a charmer, and I knew at some point I would have to have my wicked way with him. I know, how bad is that? Eventually we got around to why I was there and what the other key was all about. "Saron, you know the organisation I represent but what you don't know is the magnitude of what Fabio uncovered which he told me and said maybe one day you would need my help. They are after you because they assume you know everything, and they don't know about me". Seeing as Fabio told you everything and they are convinced I already know everything; you'd best fill in the dots".

"Ok, this all started around Nineteen forty-eight when CS came to the fore. The British ran Palestine until it was decided to give the Jewish people a part of it to form the independent state of Israel which, after what they had endured, it was considered at the

time a fair thing to do. Six
months later CS was formed
under the guise of chasing down
Nazi criminals. Initially that was
all they did but then, in 1952,
President Marak was losing at the
polls so he decided that by
chasing down families of these
Nazi's he could win the election.
He was right and won a massive
landslide. The British
government basically stood by
and said nothing, then, in 2011 it
was a disaster. CS discovered
that Lord and Lady Cawsworth
were Nazi descendants, well,
Lady Isabella Maria Cawsworth
was and by their rules that meant
Lord Cawsworth and their three
children had to perish also. On a
cold November night in 2011,
Lord Cawsworth was driving his

wife and children back from a
pantomime, they were stopped
and all gunned down. Now the
British government were in panic
mode, Lady Cawsworth was god
parent to the Queen. You can
imagine the panic that sent
through MI6. That's where
Clearmont comes in, he was
charged with sorting the mess out
and ensuring this would not
happen again. He decided to
blame the IRA, which of course
they flatly denied but it seemed
to work. Then he met with CS
and agreed a way forward which
basically let CS carry on as
before but any family members
they killed were to be done
discreetly, for this he was paid a
lump sum of money and an
income. This what Fabio found

out more for his family's
protection than anything else. He
wasn't going to get involved but
many years later when he pulled
his ace card Clearmont double
crossed him, what they didn't
expect was you". "What about
agent Fearn"? "For a few years
Clearmont was paying him
because he stumbled across the
deal with CS, I believe Fabio
trusted him over a bottle of
whisky one night and told him
about the files in Clermont's
office. Now fully implicated,
when he found out you also had
seen the files, Clearmont
instructed Fearn to kill you so
now there are two loose cannons
roaming loose". "What about the
key". "Fabio told me if you ever
came to see me, I was to tell you

everything and take you to St
Agnes in Sikkili, behind a picture
by the altar there is a safe which
you would have the key for".
"Where is Sikkili"? "It's a full
day's drive, we would need to
stop overnight Saron. Is that ok
with you"? Is it ok with me? Too
right it is, blimey this man was
bloody gorgeous. "Yes, that's
fine, thank you for helping me"
and I smiled not wanting to look
to eager.

He said we would set off at 9.00
am in the morning. I couldn't
sleep for thinking about him and,
yes, you are correct, I should be
thinking about getting out of this
mess but trust me, you should see
this man!

STUNNER FIVE

The following morning, I packed some toiletries, a pair of denim cut offs and a white flimsy top to drive there. I had on a lemon-coloured mini skirt and some sandals with little heels trying to be as sexy as I could, I wanted this man to want me like I wanted him. Nobody else was up, just me and him as we got in Jeep with the lid and doors off, it was just so hot. His eyes went straight to my legs as I climbed in the vehicle. "It's warm Leonardo". "Most definitely Saron". We chatted a bit, but it was quite noisy, and the roads weren't great. We stopped about halfway and had a cold drink. Leonardo said he knew a nice family restaurant which also had rooms so he had booked us in there and we could have a meal there that night.

I showered, well, when I say showered, it wasn't the best flow of water or very hot, but beggars can't be choosers. Leonardo was waiting for me at reception, He took my hand and led me into the restaurant, I felt like we were together as he took my seat out and sat me down.

The menu was a bit limited for me but what was coming out of the kitchen looked nice. I had a small Isle of Capri salad followed by cashew nut pasta spirals in a Romany sauce which was divine. Leonardo, being the hunk of a man he was, had oysters followed by Napoli steak in brandy sauce. It was all lovely and over two bottles of wine we chatted. He asked me how I had met Fabio and all the usual things like, how long were we together etc. He then told me that he met Oskala at a funeral, he said she didn't know but her husband had been a Russian spy and he was ordered to execute him. He said he felt so bad that he decided to look after her, he said then things happen, like they do, and she got pregnant with Sophia and because of that she had to tell everybody she was married so he just plays along with it. I was hoping I hadn't shown too much pleasure when he told me, but it certainly made things easier. We decided to have a third bottle of wine and the famous tiramisu with a brandy floater coffee. I think we both knew what was about to happen. We thanked the staff and headed upstairs, Leonardo grabbed me at the top of the stairs, kissing me passionately. "Saron, I want you, I wanted you from the day I met you. Can I make love to you"? Has Blackpool got a tower? I thought as we headed to my room. I opened the door, and he swept me up in his arms and laid me on the bed, we were both undressing each other at some pace.

I could feel his excitement as he kissed me everywhere from my neck down to my legs. He just told me to relax and let him take control which I was happy to do, he was so muscular and tanned, a proper man is what mum would have called this Italian stallion.

What would Hells Bells and Ju have thought of this hunk taking me to the pinnacle of love making. In a massive crescendo we both achieved sexual fulfillment and laid breathless beside each other. We hardly said a word afterwards, maybe he was feeling guilty or just tired, either way we both slept well. The following morning Leonardo said we should have breakfast before heading to the little church of St Agnes, he said it was forty-five minutes away. Over a nice continental breakfast, we both looked dreamily at each other. I guess we were both thinking the same thing, we had fallen deeply for each other. After breakfast, we headed for the Church of St Agnes, it stood out, it was painted white on the top of a hill, it was beautiful. I did ask Leonardo if it would be open because now in the UK, they locked them. He said of course it is open, always in Italy. He seemed somewhat surprised at my question; I felt a bit dumb. It was just as beautiful inside as it was outside. We walked towards the alter and right in front of me was the picture, Leonardo took it down and I placed the key in the lock, my heart was thumping unsure of what this could be. Inside was a large box, Leonardo lifted it down and placed it on a pew. Now it was discovery time. First of all, there was a letter from Fabio. Leonardo said he would go outside whilst I went through the box contents.

I started to read the letter.

"Saron,

If you are reading this then you have come along way but first, I must tell you from this point trust nobody and I mean nobody, this information could bring down the government and the monarchy of the UK and maybe the governments of many countries who turned a blind eye.

The files show every transaction between CS and MI6 with of course the implication of Clearmont. Also, all transactions and payments to Agent Fearn

from Clearmont. I can't tell you
where I got all this from, but I
can give you a name of a lady
should you need it. Ruth Alistein,
she is Jewish and lives in Israel.
She is a fearsome lady; all her
family were wiped out by the
Nazi, but she holds no grudges
and for many years she has been
helping families escape the
clutches of CS. She risks her life
daily and would be seen as a
traitor by her own people were
she to be discovered.

My original thought was you take
the files to a broadsheet, that way
it makes you safe and hopefully
doesn't compromise Ruth
Alistein. I think that is your
safest bet. But now you have to

get from Sardinia to London. Buy two plane tickets and don't let the box out of your sight, remember trust nobody Saron.

Good luck my love

Fabio

Xxx"

There were pictures of some of the families that had been murdered and also a list from 1952 which I assumed Ruth had logged.

I neatly folded the box down and went outside. "So, you are good Saron, you have what you need"? I could hear Fabio's words ringing in my ears "Trust nobody". "To be honest, there wasn't a lot there, just some personal bits, I'm not sure why Fabio was being so secretive". "It was the nature of the man, he used to always say "FAIL TO PREPARE -PREPARE TO FAIL" I wondered why Fabio had said trust nobody I had to assume that it included Leonardo. Had he discovered something about him but had to carry on with the plan.

We drove back but stopped at a hotel for the night where the inevitable happened. I know you think I am nuts, but I intended to fly out the next day and the likelihood was that I would never see him again. We made lust that

night, I can't say it was love. The
following day Leonardo said he
had business out of town so that
was my opportunity to get out of
the country with the box. I
managed to get a taxi and flight
back to the UK, I did what Fabio
had said and had a seat purchased
for the box next to me. On the
way I wondered if I should head
for somewhere where they
wouldn't look for me so on
landing, I hired a car and headed
for Scotland.

My plan was to tell the story to
the Scottish press then head for a
small island while all hell broke
loose. I took pictures of every
document in the box and before
heading for Scotland I placed the

box in a safety deposit box in London. I must admit it was a weight off my shoulders knowing the box was safe.

In the hotel in Scotland, I read from the pictures, it was shocking. Since 1952 there had been three hundred and fifty-eight family members of Nazi's revealed that had been executed, just because they had married, women and children, nobody had been spared and MI6 had turned a blind eye and latterly, for money. The two that stood out were Lord and Lady Cawsworth and their children and what that might stir up because of the Queen. The other was President Gilson Hawkings of the USA who died in a car crash, followed a year later by his wife and four-year-old son in a supposed boating accident. If that got into the public domain, we could kiss goodbye to the UK and US's special relationship. This indeed was a ticking time bomb and the sooner I relieved myself of what I knew the better.

It was such a lovely day, so I set off walking to the Scottish Herald offices, it was only a mile away. I arrived and was shown into a room but instead of the editor there was Paul Fearn, Gavin Clearmont and Leonardo. now I realised what Fabio had said about trusting nobody.

"Come in, take a seat Saron". Clearmont said all smugly. "I won't beat about the bush. The information we believe Fabio collated will never be published. You gave Leonardo the slip or this unpleasantry would not have been necessary, but we are where we are. These are your options, you hand over the documents and any copies you have, and we let you live, albeit you will never be allowed to speak of it. The second option is you will be named as a traitor and will be put in a mental asylum, that way, if you talk about anything, nobody will believe you because you have been sectioned. There will be no day in court, you will simply be lost in the system. You have five minutes to give me an answer or you will be taken away". "You can't do this to people". "Oh yes I can, the security of the Crown is in my hands". "You will get nothing from me". "Are you sure "? and he laughed? "Did you really think you could beat the British Secret Service? Ok, time up. I'm sure we will never meet again! Three burly male nurses strapped me in a straight jacket and flung me in the back of a van.

Chapter 8

From that point on, my life was hell. I didn't trust Clearmont, he would have had the information and I would have been murdered, of that, I was sure.

Beccerton Asylum was a red brick former Victorian

Workhouse, there were about two hundred ill people in there and about seventy male nurses which were basically guards, anybody playing up they simply stuck a needle in their arm. The bulk of the people were like zombies. The first three months I spent in solitary confinement. I had worked out who the real nutters were. There was a ginger haired woman they called Leap Year because she proposed to everyone and actually killed a nurse for laughing at her. Then there was one tooth Lenny, he was a serial killer, when they caught him, he had taken one tooth from his victims and he had a collection of twenty-seven teeth in a display cabinet, then there was Sandra, black widow, she had murdered five husbands with poison. All these people were deemed insane. It wasn't long before the male nurses gave me a pet name, "Gorgeous" that was fine by me, it kept me feeling normal, but the women guards would pick on me through pure jealously.

The days were long with nothing to do, some were given small work to do but I hadn't been there long enough for them to assess me. The experiences in this place were insane and even worse when you are a patient and not insane like the others. I think some of the nurses, as I said, I will call them that, but they were just brutal guards who drew their baton and the quiet needle, as they called it, at any opportunity.

I'm pretty sure they must have thought me being in there a bit strange. One day, I asked a nurse how I go about having visitors. She laughed and said, "Whatever you have done they have thrown away the key, you're a Category NH patient". "What does that stand for"? "NO HOPE"! she said walking away. This was the lowest I have ever felt in my entire life, but I wondered how many people the Government had done this to?

I had now been assessed and they decided to give me a job serving the food to the patients. On my very first day, this bloody nutcase came back with her tray of hot

food and kept saying peanuts,
peanuts, then she threw her food
all over me. I lost it and battered
her all around the canteen, I had
so much loathing in me she
triggered everything in me,
Finally, I felt a baton strike
across the back of my legs, and
they must have used the needle
on me. I came around to find
myself in solitary again.

I cried and cried until I had no
more tears left. I honestly felt
like I was going mad. One patient
just howled all day long, they had
nicknamed her Wolf woman, it
was so stressful hearing and
being around theses sick people, I
knew I had to get out.

STUNNER FIVE

It was now three years since they incarcerated me here and I finally was given a job in the laundry and my lucky break. Once a week a driver would come and collect sheets and all the bed linen. I was busy working when I felt a tap on my shoulder, I turned around and it was Dave Killen from my hometown of Heathcliff. "Saron, is that you"? "Dave? Yes, yes, it's me". "What the hell are you doing in a psychiatric hospital laundry? I heard you had done really well for yourself". "I did but it's a long story, I have to get out of here Dave, will you help me"? Over the next few weeks, we came up with a plan to smuggle me out in a laundry basket. Dave said the guards were supposed to check every basket, but he said they did the ones at the front but left the one's on the back.

The plan was to get me out and Dave would drop me at his flat then we would plan from there.

I was so excited; I wasn't sure I could take another day in that place. It was Tuesday morning and the nurse watching over me always went out to smoke at 10.00 am on the dot for about ten minutes so we really had to hurry.

My heart was racing as I got in the basket, eventually Dave pulled away, we had to get through. I heard Dave say to the guy. "Are you taking a look mate"? "No, I trust you mate" the gates opened, and I was out. Dave lived in Merryhill North London, he gave me the keys to his flat and said he would be back around 5.00pm.

I kissed him and thanked him. I said I would explain things and he said he would bring a Chinese home for our tea. I showered and got cleaned up the best I could, all of my belongings were at the hospital, that was money and everything. They really had done a number on me.

Dave came home with a Chinese and as we sat eating, I told him as much as I dare without going into details. Basically, I said MI6 had double crossed me and because I knew so much, they had sectioned me. I could see it was all too much for poor Dave to take in. "So, what about you? I never thought you would ever leave Heathcliff Dave". "I went on one of those singles holidays, me and Bill Gascoigne". "You mean Bamber"? "Yeah, you remember him"? "Yeah, what a pain he was, he was always twanging my bra strap when he sat behind me in class". "Oh yeah, I remember that. Also, Richard Cliff came with us, bet you can't remember his nickname Saron". "I can, it was Summer Holiday after the Cliff Richard film. So, you three went on holiday"? "Yeah, and that's where I met Sinitta"! "Bloody hell Dave, only you could get hooked up with a Sinitta"!!

"She was from down here, so I moved down three years ago but we split after six months, she went off with a postman". I started to laugh. "Sorry Dave, I shouldn't laugh. You have been a real tonic mate and thank you for getting me out of that place"".

We finished laughing and settled down to watch the news. Halfway through it came up about me. "All ports and airports are on high alert for a psychiatric patient who absconded today from Merryhill Psychiatric Hospital. MI6 have put out a high alert for this individual who is also considered to be highly dangerous, do not approach but contact this number. She is a

danger to National Security. Jan
Barnes BBC News"

Poor Dave's face. "What have
you done Saron"? "Actually
Dave, nothing personally but I
married a former MI6 agent who
they think will have passed
secrets onto me, that's why they
incarcerated me because I could
not have a trial so could not put
my case forward".

"Saron this is incredible, what are
you going to do"? "Will you nip
out and get me a hair dye, black
please? I have a false passport in
Cornwall so will need to go down
there, I have no money, they have
everything Dave". "Saron, I will
give you five hundred pounds so

you can get sorted". "You are a true friend Dave; I will pay you back once I have sorted this mess out". The following day I died my hair yet again and headed for Cornwall by train. I picked up a Pay as You Go phone at the train station and range Ju.

"Ju, I am in a real mess. I can't explain to you". "I saw something on the news Saron". "It's all BS, can you meet me in Penzance? I arrive at 3.15 pm today. Ju, can you also do me two things please? Go to my house and in the desk where the TV is, there's a fake passport with me with black hair, can you get that please? Also, can I ask a big favour mate, can you loan me five thousand pounds? I will pay you back once this is sorted. I dare not use my bank account as they will be watching". "Of course, I can I am so worried about you". "Don't tell Helen or anybody else, the less people that know the less chance they have of finding me. Love you mate". "Love you to Saron".

With that sorted I jumped on the train heading for Penzance to meet Ju with my passport and money.

The train pulled in bang on time, and I saw Ju sat in the café on the station. We hugged and both had a few tears. I told Ju the full story, everything, even the safety deposit box number and where

the box was that would create
this big problem. "Why don't you
just give it them and make it all
go away"? "Once I hand it over, I
am a dead woman walking Ju.
My plan is to get out of England
and mingle, say in Benidorm
where there will be loads of
people, then, in about six months,
contact another paper and see if I
can get them to print". "I've just
thought Saron, do you remember
Jeremy Galton? I believe he is
editor at Truth Magazine, I have
his number in my phone, he is on
Facebook". "Thanks Ju, I am
going to disappear for a while
then will try him. I might have a
better chance with him, they
won't be looking for an exclusive
from a magazine". We hugged
again and said our goodbyes. I

truthfully didn't know if I would see my bestie ever again, I really was on my own from this point. I booked a one-way flight to Benidorm. I flew through customs in Spain so was well chuffed about that. Speaking with the taxi driver I asked if there were any bar jobs with accommodation going in the town. Just as luck had it, he said his sister wanted somebody and there was a flat thrown in. Susan, his sister, had married a Manchester lad and they had a bar called Pokey Yokey, it was quite nice and so was the accommodation. Susan said to start the following night, so I had a look around Benidorm, the place was certainly vibrant.

STUNNER FIVE

The following night was my first night and it was rammed, quite a cross section of age groups, some teenagers, some mid-thirties and the rest older generation so it was nice. The girl I worked with Alexa, she was from Latvia but spoke really good English and was very intelligent.

After a month I had almost forgot why I had left England. Susan and her husband let us have a day off a week which was great, we had such a laugh, I felt re-born.

Alexa said she was going to the Canary Islands for the winter, apparently, that's what she did each year, she asked me to go with her. I said yes, it meant more time for things to settle down at home.

STUNNER FIVE

We both looked forward to Tuesday's, our day off. We'd sit by a pool getting a tan then spend the night down the town around the bars and the Sands disco at night. I will never forget the sign over the door, in big white letters it said, "THE MOST BEAUTIFUL GIRLS IN THE WORLD CROSS THIS THRESHOLD"

I guess after losing Fabio, being used by Leonardo then being locked in a nut house for three years I deserved a bit of fun, and I was going to have some. Things in Benidorm were manic, but all the workers stuck together, and we had our own little bubble we lived in.

STUNNER FIVE

Alexa was a pretty girl, they always seemed to have nice bone structure the Eastern Europeans, so it was no surprise she got lots of attention from all the males on stag parties or holidays. She said she had been married in Latvia, but her husband was killed in an accident during training in the army. She really opened up to me and I wished I could have been as honest with her, but Fabio was right, I must not trust anybody. Time flew and it was almost the end of our season. Alexa said she could get me a job as a waitress in a bar in Cost Adeje, she said she made good money, so I agreed.

What a mistake that was! I had saved enough money to pay Ju

back and had decided that after Tenerife I would contact Jeremy and take my chances.

I thanked Sue and her husband and said I would be in touch. Now for Tenerife. Alexa had gone on ahead and told me we got accommodation with the jobs at a place called the Boom Boom Club. I arrived at the centre of Costa Adeje and entered the bar, Alex met me, she was scantily clad in a black basque, stockings and very high heels, there were seven poles with girls dancing and men placing Euro notes anywhere they could get away with. It was packed, with maybe eight bar staff working the bar. Oh, this was a mistake I thought, this really wasn't for me. That

night in our pokey flat I asked
Alexa what she was doing.
"Saron, I earn enough in one
night playing up to theses losers
than I do in a week in Benidorm.
You should try it before you
knock it". She probably was
right. So, over the next few
weeks, Alexa and the girls taught
me to pole dance I was naturally
supple and fit, so it came quite
natural to me.

Instead of the bar I did the
dancing, I could make four
thousand euros in a six-day week
and because I didn't know when I
could use my bank accounts,
again, I had to get money put
aside. It became quite fun. I
suppose it was because it was all
new to me. When some

handsome hunk was placing money on me it felt quite erotic.

We had been dancing for about three months when Alexa said we should do the boat picnic thing, it was one hundred and twenty-five Euro's which included a boat to a deserted island and a champagne picnic. There were eight people on the boat which were two couples, me and Alexa, a guy called Rob and his mate Andy, both nice lads from Halifax, not particularly great looking but good fun. They flirted with us the whole of the trip. Rob with me and Andy with Alexa.

Once we were back on dry land they asked if we wanted to go for a drink with them. We both shrugged our shoulders and said

fine, let's do it. By the fifth bar
Alexa was tipsy, I was as well,
the boys seemed like they were
fine. Anyway, like all things they
said they would walk us back to
our flat. When we got there Andy
asked if we were pole dancers, he
said that he came to the Boom
Boom Club last year. When we
said we were his little eyes came
out on sticks, I think he thought
he had won the lottery!

Although I was still very
concerned about my life, once I
could speak with Jeremy, I hope
it would all work out, I still had
to enjoy my life. You know
Saron, I'm not down for long.
Anyway, Alexa ended up in bed
with Andy, but I told Rob I

wasn't like that, so he left. I think deep down I was annoyed at myself for falling for Leonardo, not in a love sense just a lust sense.

The day to totally change my life and put my head above the parapet had arrived. I rang the number Ju gave me; a lady answered. "Truth Magazine, how can I help you"? "Could I speak with the editor, Jeremy Galton". "May I ask what it is concerning"? "I'm sorry, it's a private issue". "Oh, ok, I will see if he is free, who may I say is calling"? "A friend, Saron". "Ok Saron, I won't be a moment".

About thirty seconds lapsed and Jeremy answered, "Hello, Jeremy Galton how can I help you"?

STUNNER FIVE

"Jeremy, its Saron, do you remember me"? "Blimey, that's a blast from the past, how the devil are you"? "Well, ok". "How can I help you"? "What I will tell you please do not utter to anyone". "Sounds intriguing"! "I am going to give you the biggest exclusive you will ever have".

"Now I am interested". "Could you fly to Spain to meet me"? "Um, yes, I suppose so, is it that good Saron"? "Absolutely, but you must not tell anyone, not even your wife, I trust you Jeremy and my life is on the line so please stick to the plan". "Ok, will do, I see there is a flight to Benidorm tomorrow". "I will pick you up at the airport tomorrow afternoon".

STUNNER FIVE

As I put the phone down, I knew
this was my roll of the dice, if
Jeremy tells anyone that could be
goodnight, Vienna for me so it
was fingers and toes crossed time
as I drove back to the apartment.
Both me and Alexa had finished
working but they said we could
have the apartment for another
two weeks, to be fair, they were
very good with all the girls.

The following day Alexa said she
was going to see friends so would
not be back all day which fell just
great. I picked Jeremy up from
the airport. I must have looked a
bit shocked, he really had aged,
he was almost bald with a silly
flick over like Bobby Charlton
use to do and he wore thick John

STUNNER FIVE

Lennon type glasses. This was Jeremy who used to look like Tony Hadley in his prime!

"You are looking well Saron". "Thanks Jeremy" now for the white lie, "You too Jeremy". "So, what is this all about"? "I will explain at my flat". "Ok, I am really quite excited Saron, if this is as big as you think, it could make the magazine and my career".

Back at the flat I made us a coffee and outlined my story. Jeremy just kept saying, wow and incredible Saron. We sat for over three hours, I told him I had all the documents to back up my story and, once published, I would give them to him to publish. Jeremy was so excited. "I owe you Saron, lets go and have a nice meal, my treat then I can get the 7.10 pm flight home". "Sounds good, Risotto's is nice". The restaurant was used by the locals which is always a good sign, we were seated near a window. I ordered stir fried vegetable in a falafel with salad. Jeremy had the squid which, to be honest, turned my stomach.

"So, are you married Jeremy"? "No, I lived with a girl for a long time but I'm kind of married to my job to be honest. What about you"? "No, I lost my husband, he was older than me, but I idolized him. Sadly, because of his work and his father being a Nazi, I have ended up with the shitty end of the stick as we say in Yorkshire". Jeremy laughed. "It's' really lovely to see you. Ju and Helen run a Bistro Café in Cornwall, is that right Saron.'"? "Yes and doing great". "I must make the effort and go and see them, I love Cornwall". "I'm sure, they would be pleased to see you" and shocked I thought as I said it.

Jeremy, now armed with the full story, said he would phone and email me a copy of the draft before it went to print.

After dropping him off at the airport, I decided to wander around the shops then have a few beers and an early night. I was feeling good, I just hoped Jeremy could pull this off, if not we all know the outcome.

I bought myself a little green dress, it's always nice to treat yourself if things seem good, I think. I ordered a beer at Deccies bar and sat people watching thinking hopefully, in a few days, which will be me free to go where I wanted without worrying I was about to be killed. It was the following Tuesday when I got the phone call from an excited Jeremy. "I'm sending the draft now, it's brilliant, after we publish, how quickly can you get me the documents for the follow up"? "That's not a problem, say three days after Jeremy". "If you can just approve this draft, I will publish it, this will be massive". He was making me feel excited. The internet was a bit slow at the apartment but eventually it came through. His journalism was spot on, I read and read until around 2.00 am in the morning. I could have even hugged ugly Jeremy for this. Tears were rolling down my cheeks. I emailed him a massive thank you, he must have been waiting up, he said it will be in the magazine TRUTH tomorrow and I could look for it online. With that thought I slept well and woke around 9.00 am. I went straight to the Truth Magazine site, but it was still last week's copy, I wasn't too concerned, I thought it would load up at lunchtime. I did a bit of sunbathing in the obligatory red bikini then at 4.00 pm I tried again, still nothing. I emailed Jeremy maybe six times, but he didn't come back, now I was worried. I didn't dare phone him just in case they had Jeremy or something, all I could do was wait. A day turned into two days, then five days, then a week. I was now seriously concerned. I wasn't eating, I felt sick with worry, not only for myself but for the safety of Jeremy.

On the Sunday my phone rang. "I have to say you are a tryer Saron" it was Clearmont. "We have put you through hell and you must realise that this is a wasted exercise for you. It won't be long before we catch up with you. We have the technology to lay a newspaper down anywhere in the world Iran, Iraq, China, anywhere and we can read it, so you have no chance. I am going to give you an offer turn yourself into me and come back and work as an agent for MI6 on the understanding that you sign the official secrets act and never mention any of this, that's it, you work for us and get your life back, what do you say Saron"? I hated this guy more than anyone I had ever known but we have a saying in Yorkshire, KEEP FRIENDS CLOSE and YOUR ENEMIES CLOSER so I decided to do that. "Ok, I just want my life back" I told him. "Ok, let's meet in Hyde Park on Tuesday at

STUNNER FIVE

2.00 pm, I promise there will be no funny business".

With it all sorted I was pretty sure he didn't know I had draft of the story, so I had to get my thinking cap on and decide how to play this. They had won the battle but not the war you, know me, I will revenge everybody that Clearmont and Fearn have hurt. Revenge is something in me and I'm not sure where I get it from, mum was a lovely person and dad didn't suffer fools but other than that he was a lovely man.

I decided this is one I could not win but I also know if Clearmont is true to his word then, in time, I would seek revenge, I decided to put that on the shelf for now and see if I can get my life back.

Chapter 9

I arrived back in London
wondering if I would get stopped
at immigration but so far so
good. My meeting was at 2.00
pm at a bench at the back of

STUNNER FIVE

Hyde Park Corner. I was feeling vulnerable to say the least. Everything was running through my head as I sat down ten minutes early for the meeting. I could see in the distance a man and a woman walking towards me, one was Clearmont, the other I didn't recognize. "Saron, lovely to see you" the weasel said, then he introduced his colleague. "This is Acravy Gesten, she will be working closely with you. Acravy, go and get us some coffees whilst I speak with Saron". She left and I thought, here I go. "Saron, our agreement is not valid until you return the documents. I need to make that very clear".

"Ok, you win Gavin but if that is the agreement, I only want to do one assignment for you". "That seems fair". I was surprised at that, but I suppose he was getting what he wanted. I agreed knowing I still had the draft, but I knew I needed good copies of the original documents, my plan was to give the copies to Clearmont and keep the originals in the safe box. The question was, could I pull this off? Well, if anybody could, it was me. I headed for the security box mindful they may follow me. When I arrived at the bank there was a coffee house over the road, so I sat and waited, these MI6 guys stand out like a sore thumb but everything seemed clear so I went and grabbed them. I had looked online at a company in Greenwich called Superior Copy, so I jumped in a taxi and headed there.

The guy was really nice, and he left me to it, even giving me another box to put all my copies in. I just managed to get back before the bank closed to put the originals away and, truthfully, you could not tell the difference. I booked into a Holiday Inn and sat on the bed feeling quite pleased with myself, the copies were great. The meeting with Clearmont was on Friday, then he would give me a one-off assignment and I would give him the copies.

Life at last began to feel normal, I rang Ju and Helen and told them I was in London and that I had one more thing to do which could take three months then I would explain everything. The girls were ecstatic, and I felt blessed to have such lovely loyal friends.

Was this actually it? I bet you think I am nuts and could have taken this deal a long time ago instead of being in that hospital but that's me, isn't it? Like Ju would say, I was as stubborn as a camel's backside, whatever that meant! So, my new plan was do this one assignment then maybe wait two years and let Clearmont think I had gone away then do a blog and put it all over social media.

STUNNER FIVE

Anyway, let's get over this first hurdle. I arrived at Clearmont's office, Acravy Gesten was already there, and they were drinking coffee, at that point I knew I had to have my wits about me with her, they seemed too cozy for my liking. "Ok Saron, Acravy is one of my best agents, but she is a double which you are going to need" and he pushed us both a brown envelope, it had a new passport inside, I was Kelly Logan, the instructions were to kill Agent Fearn then kill Leonardo. There was no end to Clearmont's deceit I thought. "One assignment I said". "That is one assignment" and he smirked. I hated the weasel and could not wait to one day to wipe the smirk off his face.

"Now Saron the box. I take it you have read the contents and hope you have not been stupid to make copies because they would be worthless in a court of law, they would only ever accept originals". I held my breath as he looked at each copy. "Well done, like I said, you are no longer a threat now I have the originals. This is how we are going to play this. I have sent Agent Fearn to Dublin on a trumped-up case about the IRA, if you could make it look like an IRA killing that would help. The tricky one is Leonardo; I will arrange to meet him out of Israel and will give you the details once it's finalized. I'm quite sure Acravy will keep him talking whilst you put a bullet in his head". "Simple as that hey Gavin"? "Yes, and then you are free and will never be contacted again". Although I wanted them dead for my own safety it annoyed me that he gets everything with no risk.

We both stayed in a Holiday Inn near Liverpool before flying to Dublin. She wasn't sociable at all, she didn't want a meal with me, or a drink, I was getting more uncomfortable by the hour. The following morning, we headed to the hotel where Clearmont said Agent Fearn was staying. I told Acravy I would handle this on my own, she seemed shocked but went along with it. I waited in reception and eventually Paul Fearn came down I approached him; he really wasn't expecting to see me. "Hi Paul, you look surprised to see me, fancy lunch somewhere"? He stuttered his words out. "Ok, there is a nice Italian along the coast". He wouldn't know what I was thinking but I was damn sure he was going to try and kill me! The way he looked at me I could see he wanted me so that was my advantage. While he drove, I played with the back of his neck, crossing my legs numerous times, I had him on the hook. "Paul, I missed you, can we start over? Stop the car here and make love to me on the grass". He almost crashed the car in his urgency. I got out first then, as he was getting out, I shot him in the back of the head then pushed his body into the grass and drove to the nearest town, set fire to the car and got a taxi back to the hotel.

I told Acravy to call Clearmont and tell him phase one was complete. We waited five days before Clearmont said he had set up a meeting in Morocco for Acravy and Leonardo. He said Leonardo would be staying at the Sultan Palace in Fez, he said do it in the hotel room. I was to shoot him by bursting in when Acravy was talking to him. It was all set up for three days' time, so we flew to Morocco and the city of Fez. We hardly spoke, Acravy was one strange girl. I placed a listening device in her handbag, I was certain this was set up to kill me not Leonardo. The day came and she went to room 147 and I listened. I was right, Leonardo said when I burst through the door, Acravy was to hit the floor and he would shoot me. I rang to reception and ordered room service, champagne and sandwiches. They arrived and I heard Leonardo say to Acravy, "Is this a trick"? "No, don't be silly, we have one task today and that is to kill her". They accepted the trolley and Leonardo was busy opening the champagne, I burst in and put three bullets in Leonardo's head and two in Acravy. That was it, done. I packed my small suitcase and left for the airport, and, hopefully, what would be my freedom. I landed at Heathrow and there was a problem as I showed my

passport. "One moment madam"
the guy said. I stood waiting,
when he came back, he said I had
to follow a lady into a room.

"Pease take a seat. I'm Nikki
Polston and I am an immigration
officer". "Ok, so what's the
problem"? "All I can tell you is
MI6 wish you to be detained, I'm
sure it's nothing, but the security
services do this periodically.
Would you like a coffee or a cold
drink perhaps"? "Coffee would
be nice thank you".

Now my mind is spinning, is
Clearmont going to go back on
his word because I killed
Acravy?

STUNNER FIVE

I waited almost two hours when a guy named Barry Sutton arrived, he showed me his badge and said the Head of MI6 wanted to see me. "I have your case in the car already". The customs officer gave me my passport and we set off to see Clearmont.

I was shown into his office. I had quickly put my phone on to record, I knew he wouldn't expect that. "Sit down Saron" and he handed me a large brandy.

"I sort of wanted to de-brief you on the mission Agent Fearn is dead and that has been blamed on the IRA, for Leonardo's death, CA believe it was Neo Nazis, with an MI6 agent also killed which brings me to the point, she was not part of the plan". "I realize that, but I also realised you had arranged my murder that day". Clearmont laughed, You would make a great agent, but I feel it's only fair, I have the original documents, Fearn can't blackmail me, I am free from Leonardo and Acravy, who knew the killing mission I arranged? All I have to say to you is, I hold your future in my hands, behave and our paths will never cross again". "Is that it now"? "You are free to go and enjoy your life, just stick to what I told you". He thought he had won but he didn't know Saron that was for sure.

So now I headed for Cornwall and my besties. I felt bad, I had been no help at all during the season at The Girls are Back in Town café and bistro, it was now the end of season. Helen picked me up at the train station and took me to the bistro. They sat opened mouth as I told them about my time in the hospital, the killings and the reasons why. It all sounded incredible, even I was beginning to question how this could all happen. I didn't tell the girls about the originals and my plan in maybe a couple of years of somehow getting this out and exposing Gavin Clearmont who incidentally, I dislike with so much disdain its incredible.

We had a lovely night. I said I was moving back to Polruan, and they were both welcome to live with me. Helen said the business had an incredible year so they all deserved a break and where should we go. Ju said she fancied Skiathos, Helen wanted to go to Jamacia so now they were both looking at me. "Look girls, I'm not bothered, flip a coin and whoever wins we go there". I flipped the coin and Ju won. "Ok, so Skiathos it is then. I'll book it tomorrow girls". Two more bottles of red and a delivered Chinese and we were all suitably comfortable. That wasn't the case the next day. I had a head like Gateshead and Ju hadn't surfaced by the time I left for the travel agents. Helen was of course ok and eating a bacon and egg sandwich. She said she had to take the books into the accountant in Falmouth so she would see me later with Ju if she ever surfaced, and she laughed.

There was a nice travel agent in Fowey which I liked to use. She said they had ten days in Skiathos half board leaving tomorrow night from Heathrow, so I booked it. Next, I needed to sort my hair out so booked myself in with Lynne and Gordon hairdresser, I needed to go back to blonde.

It felt so good when I came out, back to my sassy best, the next job was a new bikini and some holiday clothes. My bank account was now unfrozen, so I had money and boy was I going to

enjoy it. Four pairs of shoes, two
pairs of sandals, two bikinis, four
pashminas and six dresses plus
new make-up and I felt like the
old Saron, there was so much.
The lad on the boat across to
Polruan remembered me. "You
are that stunning girl who lived in
Polruan about three years back? I
bet you have been missing me,
that's why you came back". He
was a cheeky little bugger; he
was only about nineteen but
chatted me up all the way across
the estuary.

Back at the cottage, the girls
were all excited and started
packing. "This will be so much
fun Saron". "I think we all need
this, Helen". "Well, you certainly

do mate"! She was right, but today I actually felt like the real Saron and couldn't wait to get in that bikini and get some sun on my back.

We drove to Heathrow like three schoolgirls, singing along to summer holiday and laughing, it was the best time ever. With no delays, which was incredible these days, we were on our way and landed at Skiathos. We arrived at 11.00 pm and the shuttle bus took us to our hotel, the grandly named Hotel Marrikas. It looked nice on the outside and was beautiful inside as well. "You have chosen well mate". "Thanks Ju". The night porter checked us in and said breakfast was 7.30 am -9.30 am, they also did packed lunches if we were out for the day. He said the rep meeting was 9.45 pm tomorrow after breakfast.

We thanked him. I had room 201, Helen had 202 and Ju had room 203. The room was very clean, with the obligatory swan made from white Egyptian towels laid on the bed. We agreed to go down at 9.00 am for breakfast and listen to what the rep was selling for trips.

I enjoyed breakfast, Greek yogurt with strawberries, an apple and a nice cup of English tea. Ju had a croissant with ham and a piece of watermelon. Hells Bells threw the health kick out of the window for our table and had a full English, although I think the sausage was German, but she said she enjoyed it.

After breakfast, the rep came around with a buck's fizz each. "Hi everyone, welcome to the beautiful island of Skiathos. I am your rep for Sunny Times. I want to make your holiday as enjoyable as I can so any problems, I am in reception every night from 6.00 pm until 8.30 pm, if it's an emergency then tell reception to call Kelsey, that's me, and I will get straight over. Now a few things I need to go through, there is a safety-deposit box in your rooms, I recommend you keep your passport and travel documents in there. Here is a

form, if you could fill in your
names and contact numbers, just
in case we should need them that
would be great. Sun-cream, if
you don't have any, please buy
some, all the little shops in the
town sell it and make sure you
use it. Don't ruin your holiday by
getting too much sun. If you go
in the sea, remember, water is a
reflector, we recommend only
going in the sea for a maximum
of fifteen minutes in any hour.

Hire cars, we recommend Avis /
Green Travel and Budget, the
others quite often are not insured,
and accidents happen all the time
on these roads. If you're
considering a moped, I really
suggest you don't! I have lived

on the island for four years now and I have seen some horrendous accidents and injuries, they are really not a good idea.

Drink driving, the law is lower than the UK at 0.05% so anything over a pint of lager or a medium wine or a single spirit is your limit. They do frown on drink driving, so be warned. Ok, that's the nasty stuff, now for the nice stuff. Sail the day is a great day out with snorkeling and scuba diving and a light lunch included.

Dolphin sailing is a full day, you are taken out to a reef where you can swim with dolphins.

Night excursions. There is a trip on a disco boat to Naypa beach with a disco and a barbecue and free Prosecco all night.

Shopping excursion to Skiathos town with a meal included at the Fat Greek Fish restaurant, which is very famous, stars like Marilyn Monroe, Cameron Diaz, Matt Damon, Julia Roberts and Ringo Star to name a few have sampled the excellent menu many times.

Numbers are limited so you will need to book early to avoid disappointment. Ok, that's me finished. I will be around for another hour if you want to book anything or need anything clarifying. Thank you".

"Come on you two, let's get by that pool". We nipped to our rooms and grabbed sun cream,

books and hats and changed into
our bikinis. The pool guys looked
in amazement at the three of us
looking like Charlie's Angels as
we headed to the pool side. The
towel guys were soon there
offering towels and drinks. My
guy introduced himself to me, he
said his name was Spiro, he said
he would look after me for my
holiday. He was a nice guy,
typical Greek, olive tan, dark
hair, come to bed eyes. I thanked
him and settled down with my
book "Falling Leaves and
Mountain Ashes" by Brenda
George, an absolutely brilliant
writer, I just love her books. I
was totally engrossed in my book
so didn't see what was going on
around the pool. Helen
apparently slapped a German

tourist for grabbing her behind,
then pushed him in the pool, and
he couldn't swim so the lifeguard
dived in and saved him, there
was pandemonium. It had just
calmed down when three police
arrived and arrested Helen, so we
all went to the police station in
Skiathos, a real backward set up.
It turns out the German tourist's
mother was married to the town
mayor. This was going to be
sticky, they wanted Helen thrown
off the island, I protested that
they couldn't do that, but the
nearest British Embassy was in
Athens, so we were powerless.
Helen was in tears, they said she
would leave that night. Both me
and Ju said we would leave as
well but Helen was insistent, we
stayed and had our holiday. We

followed the police and waved her off then headed back for an evening meal. We were both upset about Helen so neither of us had much to say that night. The following morning at breakfast we discussed if we should go back and decided we should then we would take Helen maybe on a canal boat holiday. That night we flew back to the UK, but not before I gave the German a real piece of my mind.

Back in Cornwall, Helen was surprised to see us. "It's only fair mate, all for one and one for all, we are a team" I said. "Well thank you so much" and she hugged us both. "We have a surprise for you. While we were in the airport, we booked a canal boat holiday to Wales". "Really? You two are the best, when do we go"? "Day after tomorrow, it will give us time to do a bit of food shopping".

The next day we got what we needed and headed for Wales; we booked the first night in a hotel then drove to Blue Waterways to pick up the boat. As usual, the guy who I would have said was about twenty-eight couldn't believe three pretty girls had hired a boat. We did the payment thing then the guy said he would come fifteen minutes up the canal to make sure we were ok. I didn't say we had done this before. Ju and Helen said they would do the locks if I would steer the boat.

STUNNER FIVE

It is so relaxing. I just loved it. We chose a one way hire which meant we could go further. We just had so much fun, the girls were laughing trying to push the lock gates open with their behinds, Ju dropped the lock key once but luckily it didn't go in far or we would have been in a mess. We had drunk twenty odd bottles of lager before we called it a night in Llangollen, at a lovely canal side pub called Towpath Mary, apparently named after a woman coal merchant in the 1800s. We said it was only fair if we staggered the showers with there being three of us, so we tossed a coin. Ju won, then Hells Bells and unlucky Saron was up for the last shower. It didn't matter, it added to the fun, besides, you need to rough it sometimes to appreciate the good things in life mum would say. With us all ready to hit the town, we decided to try Towpath Mary to start and have something to eat. The pub was a mix of locals and boaters. Helen being Helen was soon chatting away to three lads. There was an elderly couple sat watching. "Err looks like err's having fun"! "Yes", I replied, "Are you local"? "With this accent lass? I'm a Yorkshireman and proud of it"! His wife smiled, she had a tight, blue rinse perm, you know, how the older ladies do? "Oh, I was brought up in Yorkshire". "Really, whereabouts lass"? "Heathcliff". "Well, bugger me". "George", his wife said, "Language in front of young lady". "Tha's rate Gladys, sorry love. So, what's thee name"? "Saron Leila". "Never, you are Daniel and Alice's girl, your mum's real name was Gertrude after her aunty, but she hated it I used to rib her all the time. I was a big fisherman in the day, me and your dad used to go all the time didn't we Gladys". His wife nodded, clearly bored now knowing the stories would soon be coming out.

"So, your two mates, are they Yorkshire as well lass"? "No, Staffordshire". "They wunna be a patch on thee lass. So, where you going to next"? "We are moving onto Dilley Puddle in the morning". "Oh, there is an

234

excellent park there, only about half a mile from the canal you should take a look". "So, what are your names"? "Well, I'm George Ladythorpe and this is my wife Gladys, obviously Ladythorpe". I sensed something wasn't right with Gladys when he was talking about mum and dad, and it bugged me to be honest, it was like that part of her life she didn't want to know about. I had been through so much lately I was probably being hypersensitive. "Come on Saron, Billy, Mick and Daffy are going to show us the town". "Have a nice time girls" George said, "Probably see you anyway, we are going the same way". Gladys looked the other way, there was

something she didn't like I
thought.

The three lads all thought they
had pulled but there was no
chance with me, although all
three would chance their arm
during the night.

We ended up in a club called
Lords, they were playing eighties
and nineties music, so we all had
a good thrash around. They were
nice lads but that was it, they
were just lads.

We wobbled back to the boat and
for once Helen was worse for
wear. "I'm going to bed girls;
they must have spiked my
drinks". We both laughed this
was a first.

STUNNER FIVE

With Helen in bed, we had a coffee, Ju had bought some chocolate eclairs from M and S, well, we were on holiday before you judge. "Are you ok Saron? You seemed a bit strange since you were talking to that couple in the pub. You said they knew your family". "Apparently, he was a big friend of my dad's, well they both were, but she seemed a bit odd, as if she didn't want to talk about it where he was the opposite, he was full of it.

He said they were following us, going the same way basically so I'm hoping I can get the woman on her own". "That's easy to sort, if they are in a pub with some music I'll take the old lad for a dance, that way you might get a chance to find out what the problem is". "Brilliant Ju, thank you". We finished our coffees and the beautiful cake and headed to bed.

The following morning, Hells Bells was up cooking bacon sandwiches. "How does she do it Ju"? "She has the constitution of a flippin Rhino Saron"! We both laughed as we sat down. It was really funny, Helen was singing the Gloria Gaynor song, I will Survive whilst serving Ju her bacon sandwich and me my croissants. "Hey girls, isn't this great fun? I think it's better than Skiathos so maybe it was a good thing I threw the German pervert in the pool".

STUNNER FIVE

"Right, where is next captain"? Julie said to me. "Dilley Puddle is the next mooring, apparently there is a nice park there". "Oh, blimey Saron, don't overload us with too much excitement"! and Helen laughed. "Go on you two, you might as well walk to the next lock, its only two hundred yards away". "Come on Ju, I'll race you". Ju and Helen set off leaving me happily steering the boat to the lock.

We got in the lock; Ju was quite jittery about being in the boat while the lock filled up, so she met us at the top.

It was idyllic, just steadily boating, all the fishermen were friendly and put their hands up, but I bet deep down they were annoyed that the boats possibly frightened the fish away. It was just so relaxing.

We arrived at Dilley Puddle and within twenty minutes George and Gladys pulled in behind us. The pub on the canal was called Herbert's Coal Yard, all these pubs had a story, mainly about the old canal people that worked the waterways.

We decided we would go in about 7.00 pm then have an early night. We clearly picked the wrong night; it was Karaoke Charity night. Of course, Hells Bells was in her element and Ju spotted George and Gladys. "Come over" she shouted and winked at me. "Do you sing George"? "I lass, I can sing owt that's got a medley". "Shall we do one together"? Ju asked then I realised what she was doing. They got up to do Elton John and Kiki Dee "Don't go Breaking my Heart". Ju had already sounded Helen out who by now was having a shots competition with two other holidaymakers.

I saw my chance. "Gladys, how well did you know my dad? I sensed you didn't like him and to be honest I would like to know why". She took a deep breath. "I loved Daniel, but the problem was he was married to your mum. We worked together; I was his PA". "I still sense you are not telling me everything". "Well, you should know, I was having an affair with your dad. George worked away a lot and it just happened". "So, what happened"? "It only lasted about eight months and your dad said he couldn't see me anymore. Problem was, I was pregnant with my daughter Anthea, I knew it would ruin your family, so I passed her off as Georges. Look they are coming back I'm sorry, but you should know you have a half-sister Saron, this is my number, when we get back, we'll meet you if you want"? "Ok, thanks Gladys".

I sort felt sad that dad had cheated on mum but pleased I had a sister, does that sound crazy? I guess not, you're not

surprised by anything that
happens in my life.

Back on the boat, I told the girls
what had happened. "It's like it
was meant to be Saron". "Yeah, I
know what you mean Helen, but
it feels weird. I am going to meet
Gladys; she gave me her number
so when we get back, I will call
her". "So, we might have an
addition to our team"? "Don't
know about that Helen, she might
not want to know me if she
thinks George is her dad".
"Surely Gladys has told her"? "I
honestly don't know but I do
know she felt relieved to get it
off her chest though Ju. It's
exciting but you hear all the time
about things like this going
wrong. Also, my dad is my hero,

STUNNER FIVE

I wonder why he had an affair?
He loved mum".

"Let's be honest, temptation is a
difficult one, it sounds like it was
early on in your mum and dad's
marriage, they might have had
problems early on, your
memories will be maybe five or
seven years after they were
married and maybe they were
over it and settled down". "I
know Ju, I shouldn't judge it's
just a shock".

For the rest of the canal holiday,
they never saw Gladys and
George again, maybe Gladys was
feeling she should not have said
anything, or she told George,

whichever way, that was the last we saw of them on our holiday.

We had such a super time, we laughed, we drank, maybe too much at times, and we discussed the business and how to take it forward. I still had to sort the will and everything Fabio had left me and the impression I was getting was I would once again be a very rich lady. At the moment though, my thoughts were on meeting Gladys again and hopefully spending time getting to know my sister. We had been back in Cornwall about three weeks when I plucked up the courage to call Gladys. "Hello"? "Is that Gladys"? "Yes, it is, who is this"? "It's Saron Leila, remember from the canal trip"?

STUNNER FIVE

Gladys went quiet on the other end of the phone. "Gladys, are you there"? "Sorry, yes". "You said to call so we could meet up. Can I see you"? "I am staying at my sisters in Bristol, it's a long story. Do you drive Saron"? "Yes". "Well, if you want to call and see me, my sister's house is Number 22 Columbell Way, Fromston. Bristol". "Shall I come tomorrow? I live in Cornwall so it's not a bad drive"? "Ok". "I will be there about 11.00 am Gladys". "Ok love, I will have the kettle on".

I told the girls; I was so excited but didn't understand why she was at her sisters. The following day I drove up 22 Columbell

STUNNER FIVE

Way, it was a neat, detached
bungalow on a small private
estate. My heart was pumping as
I walked up the neat garden path.
I knocked on the door and a lady
answered. "Oh, I'm looking for
Gladys". "Oh yes love, we are
expecting you, I'm Margaret".
"Pleased to meet you Margaret,
I'm Saron". "You have your
mums looks lass". "Did you
know mum"? "Yes, we went to
school together".

This was so surreal. Margaret
made us a pot of tea and she had
baked a lemon drizzle cake.
Finally, Gladys appeared, she
looked like she had been in a car
wreck, she had a black eye, her
nose was red, and she had some

scratches on her neck. I feared the worse as we sat down.

"Do you mind if our Margaret sits with us? She knows the full story". "No, of course not". "You are maybe wondering about my bruises etc"? "Yes, I did wonder". "Two days after I met you, I had told George I wasn't feeling well and wanted to go home. He wasn't too chuffed, when we got home, we sort of argued so I told him about my affair with your dad and our daughter not being his. He went ballistic. I suppose I somehow deserved it". "No, you didn't, no man should hit a woman, Gladys". "Well, I decided to come to my sisters for a while. I have carried the burden for too long Saron". "Can you tell me about dad then"? "Well, we worked to together and because George and Daniel were big fishing friends your dad got me a job in his office. You probably worked out that George is loud and quite brash, and your dad was the complete opposite, he was a kind, intelligent and lovely man.

Slowly, over the years, I guess I fell for your dad. I would see how he was so kind with your mum and my life was nothing like that. So, wrongly, and selfishly, I worked my way into your dad's life. At first, I would flirt with him when nobody was about then one day we worked late, and I cut my finger. Your dad dressed it then, it just happened, we kissed. Saron please don't think ill of your father, he was the best and when he broke it off it was because he loved your mum so very much. I couldn't compete with her in his eyes. Anyway, three months after, we split for good and I left making the excuse I wanted to go back to being a veterinary nurse. I found I was pregnant; it didn't show easily because I was stick thin in those days. Anyway, I never told your dad I had been left in no doubt it was your mum he wanted so I passed the baby off as George's, and until I met you, nobody knew, not even our Margaret did you Marg"? "No, she never told anyone". "A week ago, I went to London to meet

Anthea and over lunch, I told her
the same story, at first she was
upset with me, but she knew
what George was like, so she has
accepted it". "Did you tell her
about me"? "Yes, I told her how
we met". "Will she meet me
Gladys"? "She said she would,
but she has a high-flying job in
London, she is editor of the
Evening Gazette".

I'm sure you are thinking what
I'm thinking. I think dad was
right, if I fell in a dollop of cow
muck, I would still come up
smelling of roses. This felt like
fate, they say everything happens
for a reason. Funnily enough, I
didn't feel any animosity towards
Gladys or dad for what they did
all those years ago, in fact, it felt

great that I had a half-sister and still had family. All I could hope for was she would see me, and we got on ok.

I left Gladys, thanking her for her honesty and I said I hoped she could patch things up with George, but she answered that she didn't want too. We agreed to keep in touch, and she was going to contact Anthea and call me when she was free. I left feeling quite chipper, one, I had a sister and two, she might help me get my story published.

Back home, I told Ju and she said I had to take things slowly and not rush in expecting everything to be good from the start. That was Ju, the sensible one in our gang.

STUNNER FIVE

Chapter 10

I heard nothing from Gladys for
about three weeks. I had to go to
London, there was a letter from
Fabio's solicitor so I thought
maybe I could kill two birds with
one stone, so I rang Gladys. She
sounded quite cheery. "Have you
spoken to Anthea about a meet"?

STUNNER FIVE

"Yes, I did love, and she was very positive and its funny, I was about to ring you. She said would Saturday be ok, and she will meet you in the Heston Blumenthal restaurant in Knightsbridge? I haven't got a clue who he is, but our Anthea moves in them circles. She said 1.00 pm if that is ok". "How will I recognise her"? "She will have a white flower in a buttonhole. I do so hope you both get on Saron". "I'm sure we will Gladys and once we have done this, we can both come to see you". "Aww, what a lovely thought". "Well, I'd best go love, our Marg is taking us to Bingo". "Ok, thanks again Gladys".

Saturday soon came around. I had treated myself to a white

STUNNER FIVE

Alexander McQueen dress and
some blue Jimmy Choo shoes
and matching handbag. I arrived
in London and asked the taxi to
take me to the restaurant. "You
will like that sparrow" he said in
that cockney accent, "It's pricey
but what isn't in London
treacle"? He was a proper
cockney, and I quite enjoyed the
ride and the banter, it calmed my
nerves. The restaurant was based
in the Mandarin Oriental. I strode
in all confident, it was a lovely
setting, there were probably
thirty tables, and I could see a
striking looking lady at the far
end of the restaurant, she clocked
me. As I got closer, I could see
she had a white flower in her
buttonhole, she was very well
dressed and slim, as I got closer it

was like looking in a mirror,
other than she was a brunette.
She stood up. "Are you Saron"?
and she thrust out her hand which
had a massive diamond ring on
her finger. "Yes, I'm Saron".
"I'm Anthea, pleased to meet you
but odd at the same time". We sat
down and she beckoned a waiter
over. "I'll have a Long Island
Tea and what would you like
Saron"? "Could I have a
Hendricks Gin with soda and a
slice of cucumber please"? "Then
you may leave the menu's young
man". She oozed confidence.

"So, Saron, funny how fate deals
a hand. Mum meeting you on a
canal boat holiday then it turning
out you were brought up near
them. We would probably have

gone to the same places, but dad sent me to boarding school when I was eight, he said it would give me an advantage in the job field". "Well, from what your mum told me, he was probably right".

"Mum had a difficult life with dad, I keep saying dad and he wasn't really, was he? Anyway, he worked away a lot, mum was lonely dad was a big drinker and very loud, but you probably already know that. I'm afraid I can't bring myself to talk to him after he knocked mum about". I sat listening and looking at her, she was my double and I could see loads of dad in her. Maybe George knew all along and that's why he sent her off to boarding

school at such a young age I
thought.

She opened the menu, "Do you
want a starter"? "No, I will just
have a main". "I was thinking the
same Saron. I come here because
the vegetarian options are so
good. I hope you don't mind"?
"Not at all, something else we
have in common, I'm vegetarian
too". "Really, that's amazing".
We both ordered the same,
buttered asparagus, pink fir
potato, smoked onion emulsion
and mushroom dressing. It tasted
out of this world. Anthea said she
had a sweet tooth and was I
having a dessert. "Yes, why
not"? I went for Sambocade
which was a goat's cheese,
cheesecake with elderflower,

apple, pickled blackberries, and walnuts. Anthea had brown bread ice cream consisting of salted butter caramel, pear and malted yeast syrup. We got on really well, she said she had to go into work, but did I fancy cocktails that night at Mangos say 8.00 pm.? She gave me the address then insisted on paying the bill before leaving. I looked up Mangos and it was perfect, there was a hotel right across from it so I booked in until Monday so I could see Fabio's solicitor. To kill the afternoon, I went shopping. Well, a girl has to do what a girl has to do doesn't she? And besides, I was once again loving my life.

STUNNER FIVE

With new dresses, shoes and handbags bought, I relaxed in the hotel thinking how much we seemed alike. I rang Helen and Ju and told them how well it was going. They were so pleased.

My life felt great and if Anthea can publish what I have then my life will be sorted.

That night I walked across and met Anthea, of course, she had loads of questions about dad and our background. "Can I be cheeky? Have you got a couple of pictures of him I could have"? "Of course, Anthea. There is something I have which you could be very interested in for your paper, if you are free tomorrow, it would be best to discuss it then". "Oh, sounds full of intrigue". "Its serious stuff Anthea". "Well, today is full of surprises".

We had a lovely evening, albeit a few too many cocktails but great all the same. We arranged to meet at a café in Hyde Park. I had brought the draft to show her. Over a cinnamon bun and coffee, Anthea was engrossed. "Bloody hell, this is massive"! "It is massive but it's also dangerous until its published Anthea". "This could take governments down; you do know we will need actual proof"? "I have originals in a safety deposit box. Anthea you must not share this with anyone. MI6 will be all over his like a rash". "Look Saron, this will take me about three weeks, and we will have the story, then release the proof, then, it's game up. I will call you when I am near completion, I suggest we have different names in our phones". "Good idea Anthea, I'll have you as Jackie and you have me as Karen" "Ok, I'm so pleased we are sisters" and she hugged me and pecked me on the cheek and said she would be in touch. All I could do now was cross my fingers and hope.

The following day I visited Fabio's solicitor. His will was really thought out. He left me a house, some antique silver, almost one hundred and thirty thousand pounds and a key to a croft on the Isle of Mulgawny.

STUNNER FIVE

The solicitor said he believed Fabio owned it, but it wasn't itemized in the will, just the request for the key to be given to me. I left the solicitors more confused than when I went in but with so much going on, I decided not to go to Mulgawny until the article was released.

I caught the train back to Cornwall and Ju picked me. We had a good old natter, and she was pleased I now had family.

It was almost Christmas, and I was baking mince pies, mum taught me, and it was like a tradition, ensuring they were suitable laced with black rum, Yum- Yum!

STUNNER FIVE

It was just as I was taking them out of the oven, and I had one eye on Loose Women on the little telly I had in the kitchen when they announced breaking news.

The reporter was outside the MI6 building, a reporter from the BBC, Emma Jackson, broke the news "Today, UK head of MI6 Sir Gavin Clearmont was found hanging from a tree in Epping Forest by two cyclists who cut him down, but it was in vain. Police are saying it's too early in their investigation, but they haven't ruled out suicide or foul play. Activity behind me is frantic, rumours are rife that other international groups maybe involved. There will be a statement by the Home Secretary later today when further facts have been investigated".

My mind was now racing, had they found out about my soon to be released article with Anthea's newspaper? Was Clearmont a scape goat to clear some of the impending mess up? I rang Anthea, her phone rang but there was no answer. What had I done? Had I put my newly found sister in danger just so I could have revenge, what is wrong with me? The following day the newspapers were full of Clearmont's demise. The Home Secretary had come out and said all the signs were that Gavin Clearmont had taken his own life and no outside forces had any involvement and over the coming days, a new head of MI6 would be put in place. You know how you watch something and think they are not speaking the truth? I could see that with the Home Secretary, this was damage limitation on behalf of the British Government.

Finally, Anthea called me back. "Sorry Saron, I left my phone here and have been to see mum for a few days with her Christmas present. Have you seen the news"? "Yes, and we both know he is the patsy". "I will publish on Boxing Day so be ready for all the attention Saron, it will be relentless. If you want to come and stay with me for a few days, they won't know our connection so won't look for you here, plus,

it would be lovely to see you".
"Thank you, I will do that thank
you so much, I can't believe this
is going to happen finally". "Just
to check, you are ok with it going
to print"? "Yes, that creep's
death is just part of the crap that
the Government have put people
through Anthea. I will be down
on Tuesday if that's ok"? "Yes,
absolutely, see you then, the
brown stuff should have hit the
fan by then"! and she laughed,
and we hung up.

I could not wait but we had
Christmas Day to get through. I
was in charge of the dinner,
Helen did the veg and Ju was
doing a couple of puddings, we
decided to get a taxi to St Mawes

where we had lived and have the night at the Nettle, sorry, The Cornish Yarg was its real name.

We got there and all three of us were dressed to kill. We walked in and I didn't recognise the guy behind the bar. it certainly wasn't Barry. One of the locals said poor Barry drank himself to oblivion and this was a new couple who took over eighteen months back. They had karaoke on, and the young locals had clocked us three. Helen turned to us, "Looks like cheap night girls"! as one after another they were buying us drinks. It wasn't really affecting hollow legs Helen, but Ju was flagging. and I was feeling tiddly.

Helen pulled us both up to sing "When will I see you again".

STUNNER FIVE

We must have sounded dreadful as we finished. I had to nip to the loo and this big guy handed me a piece of paper with a number on it, I assumed he was trying to pull me, so I slipped it in my handbag, he was quite good looking in a rugged way.

The night finished with me and Ju the worse for wear and Helen singing her version of the boys are back in town, substituting girls for boys, she was so funny.

We had such a lovely night but paid for it the next day. Poor Ju looked dreadful, and I wasn't that great as Helen poured us a sherry each. "Cheers, here's to the girls. Nice breakfast for you both, full English Ju. poached eggs on toast for you Saron". Thank goodness she had cooked the eggs well.

Straight after breakfast, Ju put Christmas Carols on from York Cathedral and we opened our presents. "Oh, wow, thanks Hells Bells, I love this Alexander Mc Queen scarf and Ju, these sheepskin mittens are lovely". I got the girls a Spa Day in Truro and a Baytree handbag each, which they loved.

The day was lovely, we had a fabulous dinner, a few really nice drinks then we settled down to watch a few reruns. Only Fools and Horses Christmas Special and Last of the Summer wine then a film, "Flowers for Maria" with Julia Roberts and Matt Damon which had us all crying.

What a lovely day, we were all stuffed after the beautiful dinner, then the obligatory chocolates. Soon it was bedtime, I told the girls the day after Boxing Day I would be going to London as the article was to be published then.

On Boxing Day, we decided to head for Steinville, as the locals called it, after Rick Stein. Better known to you probably as Padstow. The area where they brought the fish in, they had tribute bands on from 10.00 am, it was my first time, but the girls said it was brilliant, it was called Cider, Pasty and Rock Festival. We arrived about 9.30 am and it was busy then. The first band up was a Suzi Quatro lookalike, she was quite good, not brilliant but ok. After she finished it was Genesis, or as they called themselves, Genamis. These were good and even looked like some band members from the actual group.

We watched a couple more bands then decided to have lunch then go back for The New Bay City Rollers which we were all looking forward to. The whole day was another roaring success. The following day I headed for London and hopefully my story in print. At St Pancras, I bought a copy of Anthea's paper and went through each page with a fine toothcomb but no joy, now I was seriously worried, so I rang Anthea. "Hi Saron, you ok, you sound worried"? "I've just bought the paper and can't see the article". "Don't worry, I was late to print so it will be in the paper tomorrow. Are you staying with me"? "If that's ok Anthea"? "Of course, I want you to". She gave me her address on Canary Wharf, and we met at 6.00 pm. I had grabbed a bottle of wine and we sat talking, mainly about dad which she wanted to know everything, which of course, she would.

I realized my half-sister was a genuinely nice person, she said George, who she had thought was her dad, had been a bully, she said he used to beat her mum so when all this came out, she wasn't surprised poor

STUNNER FIVE

Gladys just wanted some love and attention.

I realised how lucky I had been and what a special man my dad was. "What do you think the article will cause"? "Hell on Earth but as long as you have the original documents, we are safe Saron". "Well, we are safe then Anthea".

The next day I went with Anthea to the paper. The headline was, "British beauty spills the beans on corrupt secret service and British Government". The papers were running by 9.30 am and I was getting calls from Ju saying Polruan was swarming with the press and media. I told Ju to say nothing. I had to see how this would evolve. I hugged Anthea and thanked her. "I should thank you, this will make my career

Saron". "It will certainly take the fear from mine". We sat in a wine bar as all this unfolded. It came up, Breaking News, the Prime Minister is addressing the Houses of Parliament.

Richard Digby the Prime Minister.

"Members of the house, the damning newspaper article released by the Evening Gazette is not only irresponsible but downright mischievous, the young lady who gave this information was once in a mental institution and I am in no way demeaning people with mental history, you do have to wonder why now? Our head of MI6 took his own life, it has been fully investigated and I have been informed there was no foul play involved"

A back bencher stood up. "Sir, is it true we do deals with terrorists, that Saron Leila was pulled into this murky underworld because she married a retired MI6 officer whose grandfather happened to be a former German officer"?

"That is Saron Leila's story, but, come on, this is too far-fetched, are we really going to cut ties with Israel and other countries. Things can be damaged beyond repair".

Is it true you can't find Saron Leila"? "We, as a country, need to find this woman, there is no evidence to substantiate these preposterous claims. We are doing everything in our power to speak with the lady".

"What about her claims that Gavin Clearmont and Paul Fearn were on the take and thy tried to have her killed because she knew. Is this true Prime Minister"?

"The lady is a fantasist, and it appears to me this is revenge on her part, she may even be unstable".

"Order, order, no more questions, move onto other business" the Speaker of the House called.

"Blimey Saron, they are gunning for you, we need to get the proof out there. Can you get it to me this morning and I might be able to print for tomorrow's edition"? "Anthea, this bit is the most important, without this I am a nutcase on the path of revenge". "I understand Saron, they will never leave my side".

"Ok, I will have them with you around lunchtime but maybe not come to your office, reporters are everywhere". "No problem, meet me at my apartment". "Ok". Anthea left and I headed for the safety deposit box, on the way I picked up a sports bag. This is it girl, I thought, as I loaded the bag with all the documents. I arrived at Anthea's she let me in, but something was wrong, she was like shifting her eyes as if to say somebody was there. The next thing I know I have a gun in my back. "Get over there" and he pushed me towards Anthea. "So, you two think you are so clever, that you really thought you would bring MI6 and the Government down. That silly little attempt with that article will be discredited. I am here today to ensure you" and he looked at me, "Die here today, and you" looking at Anthea, "Take the blame. One will rot in prison, the other will be out of our hair for good".

Poor Anthea, what had I dragged her into? My training when I was working with MI6 made me look at his gun, he still had the lock on so his intention was to make me think he would kill me if I didn't do as he said.

I knew he would be well trained, but you know Saron don't you, he told us to sit on the bed. "This is how it will play out. I am assuming the sports bag has the incriminating evidence because Saron, you gave Gavin Clearmont copies, which was clever of you".

He went to reach for the sports bag, this was my one chance. I swung out, chopping him in his windpipe which dropped him, and I quickly grabbed his gun. Anthea by now was a shivering jelly. "Have you got any cable ties"? "Yes, I think so". "Right, do his feet and hands please". The poor girl followed my instructions to the letter, and we picked him up and put him on the bed. "Right Anthea, take the bag and publish the contents". "You stupid girl, you won't get away with it". "I will stay with this nut job and the gun. Go Anthea, go now". Anthea left and I nipped in the bathroom and put my phone on record and started asking questions.

"So, Mr. Failure, who are you". He laughed, "We will see about that bitch. I am Gerard Coulis, an agent of the British Government". "So, you thought you would kill me and put the blame on Anthea"? "I still will". "Well, you are going to struggle at the moment". "If your article runs, then massive questions will be asked, your best bet would be to cancel the article, give me the evidence and I will let you both get on with your life". "Thanks for that Gerard, all recorded so I honestly think you are stuffed". He went quiet. "Not such a big man now are you Mr. Coulis"?

We sat for almost three hours in virtual silence, he knew it was game over. My phone rang, it was Anthea. I didn't want him listening so took it in the kitchen. "We have done it sis; it will be on all the major newsstands". Anthea sounded really excited; I was too but we had to decide what to do with the chimp on the bed. I said we should drive him out to Epping Forest and dump him. "He will be too embarrassed to say two girls he was sent to kill tied him up". He had failed in his assignment so he would be pretty much toast with MI6, the embarrassment would be unbelievable.

When Anthea came home, she had a copy of the paper it was just incredible. To see what I had been through. I knew there would be interviews on TV and Radio etc.

We did what we agreed and wished Gerard all the best, leaving his hands tied but releasing his feet. He was a broken man, but I had no choice.

On the way back, Ju rang me to say there were reporters everywhere and they were hassling her and Helen. I told Anthea I'd best get back, she agreed, and we drove back from Epping Forest to her flat to get my things. A man from the BBC was camped outside the door. "Miss Leila, would you go on a TV debate tonight with the Home Secretary, the Chief of Police and the Head of UK security"? "I don't think so". "Look, get this over with and you can move on with your life. A car will pick you up at 5.00 pm and the programme will go out live from 8.00 am. Anthea said I should do it. "Ok then, I will".

I dressed conservatively; I didn't want bimbo headlines the next day from the gutter press.

They had us sat in a semi-circle, a bit like question time. There was Jackie St Clair in the chair, me, Molly

STUNNER FIVE

Ipcress, Head of UK Security, Sir Michael Holden, Home office and Greta Swincos, Chief of Police.

St Clair greeted everyone then started the debate. if you could call it that. "Miss Leila, your initial article released a couple of days ago was largely seen as the rantings of a mentally ill woman, but you have backed it up with hard evidence that not only shocked the UK but the world and one of our very important allies in Israel. I am going to ask you a question then our other panelists can try and give answers. You say you were trained by MI6 and forced to take part in undercover operations, is that correct". "Yes, one hundred percent".

"Ok, let's see. Molly Ipcress, your answer". "First of all, I would like to take this opportunity to aplogise to Miss Leila and any of her friends that were caught up in these situations. You are all aware that I have only taken this position a week ago and I am working my way through the facts in front of me, Gavin Clearmont took his own life, and you can add as much conspiracy as you wish but that is a fact. Mr. Clearmont had abused his position overwhelmingly and more is being discovered each day, to the British public, we as the UK's security barometer apologise unreservedly. On the subject of this shadowy group called The Jewish Combat Survivors Association, or CA, as referred to during these revelations. This is one for you Sir Michael Holden. This organization, and Miss Leila supplied proof, that they have systematically murdered any relative of any known Nazi war criminals, and that we have turned a blind eye, so much so that people in MI6 even took money to turn a blind eye. What is this saying about your government"? "Yesterday, when the proof was out there, I contacted the Israeli Government and they flatly deny any knowledge, they have promised me they will do an immediate search into these allegations. I agree, this is bad and the lengths that our Secret Service went to in covering up these atrocities is beyond comprehension, and we are working to put things in place so that this can never happen again".

"Miss Leila, you have sat and listened to people of intense power, what would you like to say"?

STUNNER FIVE

I cleared my throat. "I have, for many years, lived in fear of my life, my bank account was frozen, I was subjected to hellish conditions in a mental hospital as a way of keeping me from talking. I lost my husband; my life was threatened many times. I was subjected to do things for this Government that I didn't want to do. Even yesterday, a man had broken into my sister's apartment waiting for me to arrive with the proof of all this. He stuck a gun in my back and told me I would be forced to jump from the window, and he would then have my sister arrested for my murder and the proof would be burned. Luckily, I noticed he still had the lock on his gun, and I managed to attack him, we tied him up and I waited with him while the proof went to print. We then decided to drive him to Epping

Forest and release him, but we left his hands tied".

"What would you like to say about that Greta Swincos"? "Well, being honest, this part of the story appears fanciful, there is no evidence this took place".

"Can I stop you there please? I recorded it all, the man's name was Gerard Coulis" and I played the recording. Swincos was completely embarrassed by this, at the end she stood up. "I am ashamed of the Service I represent, and I formally tender my resignation from this moment" and she left. "Thank you, Miss Leila, that is, all we have time for, but I am sure over the next few days there will be more calls for resignations and, ultimately, the big prize, the Prime Minister". The lights dimmed and Jackie St Clair leaned forward. "You are a credit to all women Saron, what you have been through and still had the guts and the courage to take on the establishment is nothing short of incredible. Thank you so much for being on my program tonight. I have a driver who will take you home to Cornwall if you wish, I'm sure you want to be with friends". "Thank you, that is very kind of you Jackie, I will take you up on this offer".

I arrived back at my cottage in Polruan feeling shattered but vindicated, it was so nice to get in my lovely bed and feel safe at last.

The following day and for the next load of days, numerous things happened. The Prime Minister was forced to resign, as was the Home Secretary, a snap general election was called which saw a landslide victory for Labour so dad would have been pleased had he have seen what our corrupt government was capable of.

The Israeli Government closed down CA but would not go as far as to apologise, stating that any Nazi blood was an enemy of the state of Israel. Labour rebranded MI6 and MI5 as UK Security Service, they were amalgamated, and a new minister put in charge to oversee its work and it was to be audited every year.

My dear sister got head hunted for overall editor of the Illustrated News Group. which she fully deserved.

STUNNER FIVE

At the opening of the new season, she came to Cornwall for two weeks holiday and met Ju and Hells Bells. I'm not quite sure what she made of Helen, but I know she had some groggy mornings from our nights out!

As for we three girls, Ju was still single, Helen was with a guy who owned Grizzlies Theme Park and me, well, I would like to meet somebody nice. I had plenty of money now so that wasn't an issue, I still missed Fabio, he made a massive impression on my life. I also know I have to move on with my life. I now have a sister I never knew of so things are great.

For anybody who has enjoyed my adventures, thank you. I'm not sure if my life would warrant anymore, hopefully, I might now lead a normal life going forward but, who knows what's around the corner for any of us?

"I believe that imagination is stronger than knowledge. That our dreams are more potent than history. That belief is more powerful than facts. That hope always triumphs over despair That laughter is the only cure for grief. And I believe that love is what we all wish for."

Saron xxx

If you have enjoyed this book, please take time to see my collection of forty-seven books so far written, all on Amazon Worldwide in Paperback /Kindle and most now on Audio.

STUNNER FIVE

Please check out my website
www.colingaltrey.co.uk

Instagram: **thepeakdistrict author**

You Tube: Colin J Galtrey

Facebook: Colin J Galtrey (Author)

Printed in Great Britain
by Amazon

84637596R00169